Hooked

Books by Jane May

DOGGY STYLE

HOOKED

Published by Kensington Publishing Corporation

Hooked

Jane May

KENSINGTON BOOKS
http://www.kensingtonbooks.com

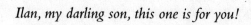

Ilan, my darling son, this one is for you!

Acknowledgments

First and foremost, much gratitude to the brothers Jacob and Wilhelm Grimm for writing "The Fisherman and his Wife," the original fairy tale upon which *Hooked* is based.

I'd also like to acknowledge (with much flourish) the following people:

Joel, the number one man in my life (aside from my dog, Miles) for his choice lines, guy advice and incredible patience; Ted Okie, "nautical" editor, wooden boat master craftsman and my son's sometime drinking partner; the talented Dianna Craig; Marc Lawrence; Derek Cohen; Captain Jim O'Neil; Mabel Miller (never give up the fight!); Mara Maunder (you're such an inspiration to me!); Steve Schustack (owner and operator of www.fort-lauderdale-marine-directory.com); Sean Murphy, comedian and another of my son's drinking partners (check out his website at www.seanmurphy.org); the ever informative Peter Matthews (president of the *Sonar* Association on the Isle of Wight, UK); Marilyn Horowitz; Dr. Alan Creed; Dr. Bill Sharfman; my terrific webmaster, Jack Passarella; Melissa and Rene Diaz for hiring a certain Romanian assistant at their salon; Steve Haas and Eddy Ramos of the China Grill, Miami; my dear cuz, Howard Harrison (thanks for the "bread" and board!); Dr. Alice Dibenedetto (for keeping me centered); Kim and Frank; Anne and Harry Schnell; Dorothy Most; Andy Watkins (whoa—two books, who would of thunk?); Ariel Morejon; Vera "Snowbird" Chatz; Lillibet Warner of Caldwell Banker in Key Biscayne; Ilioara Diaconu; Ernie Ku; John Loche; Robert Tronz; Terry Peters and the *Isle of View*; Tony Walker of The Coral Reef Yacht

Club of Coconut Grove; the squash courts of The SportsClub/ LA (sweaty Eddie, you're my hero!) and my ever-indulgent squash partners: Leslie, Paula, Heather, Ellen and Janine; Carl Hiaasen (my idol and inspiration); my ever-patient editor, John Scognamiglio; Kristine Mills-Noble of Kensington for her terrific cover design, as well as everybody else involved; and lastly, my delicious agent, Evan Marshall. What would I do without you?? Flip veggie burgers? Tons of kisses to my parents and my daughter, Ris.

The following sources were also invaluable: *Time Out Miami*, *Ocean Drive*, *Vanity Fair*, *Woodenboat Magazine*, www.askmen.com, www.edmunds.com and *The K.I.S.S. Guide to Sailing* by Steve Sleight.

P.S. This is a work of fiction and the characters (despite some similarities to those aimlessly wandering the earth) are well, you know, fictitious. Except for Mr. Donald Trump who I hope will indulge me for putting words (of wisdom, of course) into his mouth.

"You must know the sea and know that you know it and not forget it was made to be sailed on."

—Captain Joshua Slocum
Sailing Alone Around the World

Prologue

Once upon a time in a faraway kingdom bursting with strip malls, luxury high-rises and enough bling to stretch across the Atlantic Ocean and back, Raymond Prince prepared to anoint a royal consort in the backseat of a cobalt blue Mercedes sedan.

With a full moon as his guide, Raymond unhooked the front-loading brassiere of his target market and chuckled to himself. Damn, if those tan-lined double Ds didn't remind him of the headlights of an eighteen-wheeler!

"Nothing like the feel of genuine nappa leather seats against bare skin," he said to the redhead whose name he'd forgotten after the second round of drinks. "So luxuriously sensual and soft, eh, babe?"

"Oh, yes," she replied, giggling. "But, Prince, you're, you're so, so . . ."

"Ready to drive a *hard* bargain, perhaps?"

Raymond sucked in his gut and had just unbuttoned his jeans when the echo of footsteps—specifically, high heels walking in a slow, determined gait—caused his gear shift to malfunction and his heart to sputter like a waterlogged engine.

The cause for his alarm was well founded. At this hour, the dealership had long since been locked and blocked. Nobody was permitted on the lot except for his security guard, Jorge, and he sure as hell didn't own any stilettos.

"What was that?" whispered the redhead, failing miserably to cover her breasts with the palms of her hands.

"Probably nothing, babe, but let the Prince here check it out."

Raymond slowly opened the car door, slinked out the side and peeked over the hood.

The news was not good. In fact, when he discovered the identity of the mystery guest, he clenched his perfectly veneered teeth with such force he nearly cracked his left bicuspid. He tried to duck for cover, but alas, it was too late.

"RAYMOND!" shrieked Sandy, his wife of twenty years.

Despite her petite stature, Sandy possessed the demeanor of a heavy-weight wrestler with the vocal chords to match.

"YOU LOUSY SON OF A BITCH BASTARD!"

"It's not what you think, honey. I was closing a deal here."

"With your fly open? Who the hell do you think you're kidding?"

And just like that, Raymond Prince, the successful owner/operator of a string of used car dealerships throughout Broward and Miami–Dade counties, saw his bank accounts go up in flames.

No more private lap dances at five hundred bucks a pop. Ka-ching!

No more custom-made suits from Milan. Ka-ching!

No more gambling junkets to Paradise Island and penthouse suites at the Atlantis. Ka-ching!

No more fifty-yard-line season tickets to the Dolphins or box seats to the Heat. Ka-ching, Ka-ching . . .

KERPLUNK!

"It won't happen again, honey," he cried, pulling at his salt-and-pepper combover. "I promise I'll change."

"You're damn right you will!" shouted Sandy. "Like you would never, ever, in your wildest dreams imagine . . ."

Little did Raymond Prince know he was about to take a swim with the fishes.

Literally.

Chapter 1

From the moment of impact, twenty-eight-year-old Clarence "Woody" Woods was hooked.

Both line and sinker.

He hardly flinched when that tray of mojitos cascaded onto the front of his khaki shorts and soaked clear through to his skin.

Nor did he squirm when the concoction of rum, lime and sugar leaked down his legs and pooled inside his Top-Siders, causing his toes to stick together and every synapse in his body to short-circuit.

Nope, Woody just stood there in the middle of the Spinnaker Café. Frozen stiff.

As the temperature in Miami hit ninety-two degrees.

"I am so sorry," whispered the beauteous vision before him. "Shame for me! I am shit waitress for sure."

"No, you're not at all," he said. "This was all my fault. I was spaced. Totally not looking where I was going."

But the truth was that Woody, who had worked at the Trade Winds Yacht Club on and off since his preteens, could easily navigate every square inch of this exclusive facility. Blindfolded. But of course that was before a girl with huge Caribbean Sea–glass eyes and long auburn hair so disoriented the poor sailor, he slammed into her with the force of a tsunami.

"But look what big mess I have made of you now," she said, pointing to his crotch.

And just like that, Woody's six-foot frame shrunk to the size of a pea. His soggy clothes left behind in a pile amongst plastic glasses, ice cubes, salted nuts and what little remained of his dignity.

No sooner had Woody made a very speedy exit from the Spinnaker Café, than the competition arrived.

Armed and ready.

Judging from their battle fatigues, these twenty-three year-old boys clearly worshiped the preppy gods of entitlement. Pastel-colored Lacoste shirts worn loose. Collars popped upward. Abercrombie and Fitch cargo shorts, slightly frayed. Prada flip-flops. Rolexes. Vuarnet sunglasses.

In other words, all the best their parents' money could buy.

Todd Hollings, the taller of the two by several inches, zeroed in on the new addition to the club's wait staff. With those tits, long legs and cinched waist, her body reminded him of his younger sister's Barbie doll—the one he used to secretly borrow for jerk-off sessions in the bathroom.

Todd turned to Barry Felds, his best friend since grade school. "Dude, get a look at that premium piece of ass."

"Daa-aaam," came the equally profane observation. "That girl is so fine!"

The boys sauntered up to the hostess. Before she doubled her weight in saddlebags, Todd used to think Babette was pretty hot for an older woman.

"Will you handsome devils be dining with us today?" she asked.

"Absolutely," said Todd, mentally disrobing a certain waitress scurrying past him. "But no need for a menu. I already know what I want."

The Trade Winds Yacht Club sat on a jut of meticulously landscaped grounds on Biscayne Bay within walking distance of the town of Coconut Grove. Its facilities, fine-tuned year after year, were top-notch. Some seven hundred strong members had access to a Mediterranean-style clubhouse with a formal dining room suitable for large parties, as well as the Spinnaker Café, an indoor/outdoor bar and grill, a large pool, a ten-person Jacuzzi and two tennis courts.

The Trade Winds marina offered one hundred and thirty slips with enough draft to accommodate sail as well as power boats up to sixty-five feet. Not to mention every amenity a picky boater could desire from 50-200 ampere electric service to individual pump-out stations.

Despite the usual drama associated with running a high-class establishment like the Trade Winds Yacht Club, Woody enjoyed his job. On this particular day, however, he wished he'd stayed home.

It was bad enough that he'd smashed into that new waitress with every diner in the café as his witness, but to have bolted from the premises with his tail between his legs? That was just unacceptable. Especially for a guy whose reputation around the club had been built on his strength of character, professionalism and an ability to stay cool in dicey situations—on and off the water.

He should have just laughed off the incident and then offered to help clean up the mess for which he was responsible. Period. That would have been the proper move to make.

Still chastising himself, Woody was just about to slip on a clean polo when his boss, Skip Edwards, lumbered into the staff locker room. Farting loudly with each step taken.

"Knew I shouldn't have had that fucking chili," he barked under his breath.

With his retirement only a year away, Skip's moods were often less than sanguine.

"Hey, boss," said Woody.

"Glad to see you're still alive," said Skip, his beef jerky face softening. "I was worried about you, son."

He placed a gnarly, baseball-mitt-sized hand on Woody's left shoulder.

"Old man Dixon told me he saw you running from the café like your balls were caught on fire."

Woody felt the skin on his cheeks sizzle. The way dirt flew around the club, his boss must have heard what had happened.

"It was nothing . . ."

Bullshit, it was huge. He had no idea who that waitress was or where she came from, but he'd never reacted to any girl in that manner before.

". . . Just a minor accident, that's all."

Skip pointed to the soggy clothes on the bench and laughed. "You mean to say, you pissed yourself?"

But before Woody had a chance to concoct an explanation, his boss took off for the bathroom.

"Just remember, son," he called over his shoulder. "I'll leave you with one piece of valuable advice. Beware of pretty girls bearing drinks."

Woody returned to the marina in time to witness Frank Elliot backing his forty-two foot diesel-powered pride and joy, the *Nautical but Nice*, into his slip.

Elliot's wife stood at the bow. Boat hook in hand. Picture perfectly still, save for her blunt-cut highlighted tresses blowing in the breeze.

"What the hell are you waiting for!" shrieked her husband, so loudly his second mate nearly lost her footing. "Get the damn starboard line already, Louise!"

Mrs. Elliot looked left, right and then up toward the heavens for support.

"Help!" she whined.

With the *Nautical but Nice* inches away from the freshly waxed hull of a neighboring sloop, Woody knew he had to act fast.

"The right side, Mrs. Elliot," he whispered loud enough for her to hear but soft enough so her husband wouldn't.

The woman mouthed a thank-you to Woody and proceeded to pluck the correct line off the correct piling. In her excitement over a job well done, however, she managed to drop the rope into the water. Lucky for her, Mr. Elliot was busy tying off the stern and didn't see this egregious mistake.

"Now what am I supposed to do?" Mrs. Elliot moaned. "Frank is going to kill me. This is exactly why I hate coming on the boat. Man turns into a regular Captain Bligh."

Silently and effortlessly, Woody reached for a stanchion and boosted himself onto the bow. He borrowed the boat hook from the flummoxed female and fished the line out of Biscayne Bay on the first try.

"Can you take it from here, Mrs. Elliot?"

"I, I think so," came the unconvincing response.

With the boat still shifting in its slip, Woody decided it best to stick around to make sure Mrs. Elliot tied off the cleat without incident. He recalled the time Mr. White's "secretary" had not been so careful and ended up being rushed to Mount Sinai Hospital.

The severed tip of one of her perfectly manicured digits packed in ice.

It was a messy situation.

And an even messier divorce.

Woody pocketed the ten-dollar tip Mrs. Elliot insisted he accept and then ran off to help Mrs. Burke transport her groceries to the vintage trawler she shared with her husband. She being Irish and he Jewish, their boat was aptly named: *Mixed Nuts.* But after fifty years of marriage, the "Bicker-steins"—as the couple was secretly known amongst staff members—had managed to switch ethnicities.

"Thank you so much, dear," said Mrs. Burke. "My arthritis is really slowing me down today."

"Sorry to hear that," said Woody.

"I must look like a hundred and ten. An alter kaker."

Woody assumed this was a less than complimentary description and insisted she looked like a teenager.

"What a sweetheart this boy is! Still nobody special yet, huh?"

"Nope, afraid not, Mrs. Burke."

"I can't believe you don't have a special gal. Such a face this boy has. You look just like John F. Kennedy, Jr. Anyone ever tell you that?"

Woody smiled. "Just you, Mrs. Burke."

"You know, my mahjong partner, Ida, she's got a gorgeous grandchild and—"

"Anne," interrupted her spouse, who suddenly appeared in the cockpit, glass of whiskey in his hand. "Will you leave the poor kid alone? Every week you ask him the same question, and every week he gives you the same answer."

"Such an expert on the opposite sex, that one is. Mr. Lance Romance. Besides, who wanted your opinion, Harry?"

"And who gave you permission to play Yente the matchmaker?"

Woody cleared his throat and began to pass Mrs. Burke's shopping bags to her husband.

"What the hell did you do, Anne? Buy out Publix?"

"All to support that fat gut of yours, Harry!"

"Guess you haven't noticed your fat ass in the mirror lately, huh, honey?"

"Excuse me," said Woody as he handed off the last parcel. "But is there anything else I can do for you folks?"

With a skirmish brewing, a speedy departure from the battle-field was mandated.

"No, thanks, son," said Mr. Burke. "But if you see Ariel, could you tell him my damn head is on the fritz again."

"You can say that again," snickered Mrs. Burke, pointing to her bald husband.

On that sour note, Woody bade the lovebirds adieu and had just turned to leave when the Hammond twins—Christopher and Jasper—charged up the dock toward him. Accompanied by their recently separated mother, a very attractive forty-some-thing blonde with legs as long as the Amazon and a reputation equally as treacherous.

"Hey, dude," said Christopher, giving Woody a high five.

"Hey, dude," echoed Jasper, his mirror image, save for brown rather than green eyes.

The twins, Jasper and Christopher, were in Woody's youth sailing group and yearned to become Olympic racers. After they captured gold for their country, they planned to attend Yale like their father, play major league baseball, become firemen, open up a chain of video game stores and then travel to Mars.

"So, don't keep me in suspense," said Woody. "How'd you guys rank today?"

"We totally kicked butt!" said Jasper.

"Exceeded all expectations," added his brother, the more cerebral of the two.

"Awesome," said Woody. "This was your most challenging regatta yet."

"But their success is all thanks to you," said the twins' mother, smiling. "The best and, I might also mention, the most adorable sailing coach anyone could hope for."

Woody chose to ignore the latter comment and addressed the former.

"Your boys made it easy for me, Mrs. Hammond. They're terrific students. Eager and super enthusiastic."

"Too bad they don't have the same attitude toward their homework."

"Aw, Ma," sighed Jasper. "Can you chill?"

"Yeah," piped in his brother.

"By the way," said Mrs. Hammond. "The boys want you to come to their birthday party next Saturday night at our house. I promise it will be fun for kids as well as us grown-ups."

Given Mrs. Hammond's bad rap sheet, Woody thought it wise to decline this invitation. Especially since the club had un-spoken rules (often broken, of course) about staff canoodling with club members. Not to mention those members whose hus-bands—ex or otherwise—happened to sit on the governing board of directors.

"We'd really love to have you, Woody," said Mrs. Hammond, licking her chops.

"Thanks, ma'am, but I've already got plans."

"A hot date or something?" asked Jasper.

"See you two monkeys next week," said Woody, choosing to ignore the question.

He took leave of the twins and their mama, and headed for the dock house, a small, gray shingled shack at the very end of the main pier. It was there that Woody found his boss hunched over his cluttered desk, slurping coffee and chewing on an unlit cigar which his doctor had forbidden him to smoke.

"Fucking paperwork," grumbled Skip.

"You know. It'd be much easier if you'd let me teach you how to use the computer."

"I'm afraid it's too late to teach this old salty dog new tricks. Which reminds me, that new member, Ted Page . . ."

"You mean Fred Sage," said Woody. "His Bertram 450 gets delivered this afternoon."

"Yeah. And from what I've been told, damn fool don't know his ass from his bowline when it comes to boats. Never even owned a canoe before."

"Terrific, I can hardly wait to meet him."

"Well, here's your chance, son. Seems the boat is already in the channel and Mr. Terrific has just pulled into the parking lot. As for me, my hemorrhoids and I got an appointment with the proctologist."

Fred Sage may have flunked out of community college, but he was far from dumb. A New Jersey transplant, he immediately honed in on a by-product of South Florida's booming real estate market and started a company that delivered home insurance for the average buyer. Hassle-free. Cheap. With fast, reliable payouts. Or so his ads claimed.

Now, in the good old days, a guy like Fred Sage would never have been able to secure membership at the Trade Winds, a club established in the fifties by a group of stodgy old yachtsmen and favored by many wanna-be social climbers in the greater Miami boating community. But times they were a changing. Old money was dying off and, as former club commodore Gregory Cox so delicately put it, "The current economic climate sadly dictates a softening of standards."

And so it came to pass on this particular Sunday afternoon in late January, this same Mr. Cox, along with his withered cronies, Mr. Collier and Mr. Duke, had gathered on the dock to watch Fred Sage's forty-five foot Sport Fisherman, the *Midas Touch,* back into its newly assigned slip.

"I heard the guy struck it rich practically overnight," explained Mr. Cox, pulling at his septuagenarian jowls.

Mr. Duke pursed his lips and shook his head. "Probably some illegal scam."

"Yeah," agreed Mr. Collier. "Like dealing pharmaceuticals."

Mr. Cox widened his eyes. "Word is the boat was bought for a pittance off some Columbian who needed to unload it real fast. Nearly factory fresh. Less than a hundred hours. Fully loaded. Lucky bastard."

As if on cue, Fred Sage, the "man of the hour," was hustling up the dock in his bright plaid Bermudas, a red Polo and fresh-out-of-the-box Top-Siders. A few steps behind him was his fiancée, Trish, a former "swimsuit model" who under normal circumstances would never have given this middle-aged munchkin as much as a sniff. She was dressed for the occasion in her fresh-out-of-the-box four-inch stilettos, neon blue short-shorts and a pink tank top across which ran the rhinestone letters "r-i-c-h-b-i-t-c-h."

"Fred, can you please slow down? I'm going to—SHIT!" shrieked Trish as the heel of one of her strappy metallic Manolos plunged in between the wooden planks and snapped off.

"Didn't I tell you not to wear those shoes?"

"What the hell do you know about fashion?"

"Enough to pay for the bills you run up at Neiman's, honey bunny."

"But now what am I supposed to do?"

"Walk barefoot, perhaps?"

Trish, clearly miffed, had no choice but to heed Fred's advice.

"Why did you make me come here anyway?"

"Please don't whine. It's not your most attractive quality," said Fred. "I wanted you to come see the boat I bought for us."

"But I decided I'm—I'm seasick."

"Seasick? You're joking, right? We haven't even left the dock!"

Several yards away, Mr. Cox, Mr. Collier and Mr. Duke observed the couple with great interest. Like a modern-day Greek chorus, the men sang their disapproval in varying pitches of disgust.

"Sweet Jesus," exclaimed Mr. Duke. "If those clowns get any louder . . ."

"They'll break the sound barrier!" said Mr. Collier, taking the liberty of finishing his friend's sentence.

"Only goes to prove," piped in Mr. Cox. "You can take some people out of New Jersey, but you sure as hell can't take New Jersey out of some people!"

Because Misters Cox, Collier and Duke—all plagued with hearing problems they refused to acknowledge—voiced their opinions in less than dulcet tones, Woody, who'd just finished securing the lines of the *Midas Touch*, was privy to their conversation. It came as no surprise to him that the "Geezer Patrol" would slice, dice and convict Fred Sage before actually meeting him.

If Sage's reputation preceded him, the same could be said for his and his fiancée's colognes—a fusion of scents like coconut, musk, bubble gum and a forest of lilacs. Woody also wondered whose diamond reflected the sun with more intensity—the rock on the girl's finger or the equally big stone adorning Sage's ear. But as he was about to switch into his ambassador mode, he needed to keep objectively focused.

"Mr. Sage?" he said.

"Live and in person, I'm afraid," said Fred.

"I'm Woody, the assistant dockmaster. I'd like to welcome you to the Trade Winds Yacht Club."

"Thanks, bro," said Fred, shaking Woody's hand. "The pleasure, I hope, will be all mine. Certainly cost me enough to join this friggin' joint. Jesus, will you get a load of this friggin' tub of mine!"

"It is quite a boat, sir," said Woody.

"No shit! Gonna cost a small fortune to fill up the tanks!"

Personally, Woody had no sympathy for anybody dumb enough to buy a gas-guzzling, noise-polluting stinkpot like that.

"Had no idea this boat was gonna be so friggin' big."

"Pardon me," said Mr. Collier. "I'm not sure if I understand. How could you make a costly purchase like this sight unseen?"

"Well, I did see it. On-line. Bought it on *Craig's List*."

"What the devil is that?"

"It's a Web site on the Internet, Mr. Collier," said Woody. "Kind of like an on-line bulletin board for all sorts of things."

The concept was too obtuse for him to grasp and only served to make the grumpy old man more grumpy.

"How could you possibly buy a boat from a photograph?" asked Mr. Duke, ruffling his unibrow.

"People do it all the time," said Fred. "Bought my Porsche and Trish's Beemer on-line, too."

Woody watched Mr. Duke roll his eyes at Mr. Collier, who in turn rolled his eyes at Mr. Cox.

"But you gentlemen can't deny Mr. Sage has found quite a beauty," he said, doing a quick course correction to avert a collision.

"Gee, thanks," piped in Trish, who up until now had been deeply involved with text messaging on her phone.

"No offense, honey bunny," said Fred. "But I think Woody was referring to the *Midas Touch*."

The girl sneered at the vessel and then back at her fiancé. "Oh, excuuussse me. So what exactly are you trying to tell me, Fred?"

"Hey, come on, who thinks you're the most gorgeous gal around?"

"I don't know. Who?"

"Allow me to demonstrate."

And with that, Fred pressed his mouth to Trish's and held steady. Woody pretended to check out a hangnail while the Geezer Patrol snickered amongst themselves.

"Oooh," said Trish when she came back up for air. "Now I gotta pee. That iced coffee ran right through me."

Woody suggested she use the head on the boat.

"Like what's that supposed to mean?"

"The shitter," said Fred, whose red-stained mouth failed to make him more attractive. "Excuse my French. The head is nautical lingo for toilet."

"Well, if it's all right with you," said Trish, "I'm gonna use a real bathroom. One that's on terra fema."

"Firma," corrected Fred. "As in your sweet ass, honey bunny."

"Whatever."

And with that, the girl scurried off with all six eyes of the Geezer Patrol fixated on her perfectly rounded posterior.

Fred motioned to Woody. "Come on, bro, what say we check out this baby?"

"Ah, sure," said Woody, caught unawares.

The Geezer Patrol awaited an invitation as well, but when none came, they all retreated to the club bar for their gin and tonics.

Fred, meanwhile, nearly lost his footing while boarding the *Midas Touch*.

"You know a lot about boats and shit, right?"

"Well, yeah, I suppose," said Woody. "Spent most of my life on the water."

"Me, I grew up in East Newark. Near the scenic Hackensack River. Nothing but trash, industrial waste and floaters in there. Speaking of which, I'd like to make you an offer you can't refuse."

"I'm not sure if I like the sound of that proposition."

Woody wasn't much of a movie buff, but he did recognize

that legendary quote from *The Godfather*. He'd watched the film on TV one night when he couldn't sleep.

"Hey, relax. Just love using that line. Always gets the customer's attention. Here's the deal, bro. I'm sure there's not much to driving a boat like this, but," he said, lowering his voice, "the problem is Trish thinks I'm some kind of fucking expert yachtsman. And before she catches on that I really don't know shit and chews me out for blowing all this money she could be spending on herself, I gotta get me educated. Fast. Your boss says you're a top-notch instructor, so I'm thinking you might just be my main man."

"Ah, I teach sailing to kids, Mr. Sage."

"Fred, call me Fred."

"Don't mean to disrespect or anything, Mr. Sage, I mean, Fred, but why not ask the guy who delivered your boat to help you out?"

"Not available. With his brother away on an extended vacation, if you get my gist, this joker, well, he's *el splitso* tomorrow. Hopping on the mule train back to Central America."

"Oh, I see."

"Listen, I hear you got Mondays off."

"Most of the time."

"I also heard you could use extra cash."

"Well, yeah, can't argue that point."

Woody didn't feel like getting into a long discussion as to why. Especially because he'd promised Mr. Vargas he'd help rig his new sail and he was already fifteen minutes late.

"How about this? I'd be willing to pay you three hundred big ones to spend tomorrow cruising around with me. We can position it as a, well, you know, a fishing trip. So whaddya say, bro?"

Three hundred dollars, thought Woody. That amount of money would pay for more than half of that Garmin GPS system he needed to buy.

Fred Sage was right. He had made him an offer he just couldn't refuse.

Woody tried to scurry past the back door of the Spinnaker Café unnoticed, but Elizabeth Vega, daytime chef and wife to Ariel Vega, the club's mechanic, caught him in the act. Hell, that woman could see an ant doing a backstroke in the middle of the Atlantic.

"Don't you be sneaking off like you didn't see me, child!" she shouted, wiping her hands on her stained apron.

"Sorry," called Woody. "Spaced. Been a long day."

"So dis be an excuse not to come give me some lovin'?"

Woody hustled over to Elizabeth for a hug. She smelled of her famous Jamaican conch chowder and jerk chicken.

"You be hungry?"

Had she heard his stomach growl?

"Nah. I'm fine."

"Don't you be lying to me, child. I happen to know you didn't eat lunch today."

Before Woody had a chance to explain, let alone escape, Elizabeth ferried him inside. The kitchen was empty save for Luis, the Costa Rican dishwasher, dancing at the sink. But he was clearly too into his music on his iPod to either care or notice he had an audience.

Elizabeth whipped up a fresh Cubano within a flash. One bite of the pressed sandwich—slow-roasted, citrus-flavored pork combined with ham, dill pickles and Swiss cheese—sent Woody's taste buds into gastronomic ecstasy.

"Now, don't you go anywhere, 'cause I got a surprise for you."

And with that Elizabeth disappeared through the swinging doors into the café. Woody was so busy stuffing himself he never considered the notion that she might be up to no good. But when she returned moments later he nearly choked on his food.

"Woody, dis here is Madalina," said Elizabeth, impishly grinning. "I thought you just might like to meet her all proper-like."

The girl had changed out of her navy miniskirt, Trade Winds logo white collared shirt and sneakers into a pair of jeans with a frayed hole on one knee, a pink tank top and flip-flops. Her hair hung loose, halfway to her waist. Freshly showered, it was still damp.

"Hello, Voody. Is pleasure to see you again."

There was a sliver of a gap between her two top teeth which Woody found sexy. As well as every inch of her.

"Ah, likewise."

He instinctively extended a hand to shake hers. Too late to check if his palm was sticky from pork or pickle juice or for that matter, nerves.

"I must say to you again how so sorry I am for making mess of you," she said, returning the gesture.

Her fingers were small and childlike, but her grip was as strong as a grown man's.

"Hey, seriously, it was all my fault."

"You know," said Elizabeth, butting into the conversation. "Dis boy, he is such a gentleman. De nicest boy you ever wanna to know. Everybody love dis boy. He is some catch, dis one be. And, you know, dis boy, he gonna sail his boat 'round the world by hisself some day."

"Elizabeth, I realize you've got my best interests in mind here but, no offense, could you cut the sales pitch?"

"Not saying anything that ain't true, but don't you worry none; it's time for Elizabeth to get home to her other children."

"I think she love you very much," said Madalina after Elizabeth had left.

"She's had this mother thing going on with me since I was twelve, but sometimes she embarrasses the hell out of me."

"Is because she is proud for you."

Woody shrugged his shoulders and said nothing.

"So tell me, you will really do such a big sail?"

"If all goes according to plan, yep."

But at this particular moment, the trip Woody had spent so many years preparing for wasn't exactly on his mind.

"You are very brave."

"Dunno about that. Some people call solo sailors crazy, but the fact is, a crazy man wouldn't be able to navigate his way out of a harbor. Let alone sail across oceans. Anyway, my dad, well, he was quite an adventurer. Guess it's in my blood."

"Adventurer?" she asked, mangling the pronunciation. "I do not know this word."

"Someone who, well, takes risks. How can I put this? An adventurer is someone like Christopher Columbus. He took a risk when he sailed across the ocean in search of new worlds. Or when Sir Edmund Hillary climbed Everest. Nobody had ever climbed to the summit of that mountain before, so it was considered, well, you know, a huge risk. And so guys like that are considered adventurers. Explorers."

Despite his explanation, Madalina still looked quite confused.

"Forgive me, but my English is not very good looking."

"Sure, it is. It's—it's beautiful."

Had Woody actually allowed those words to drop out of his mouth?

"I try hard to study my English fast. I watch television and I make collection of many American magazines. I like very much *Vogue, Peoples, InStyle, Town and Countries, Ocean Drives.* Many, many stories of rich and fame."

"Plenty of that in South Florida."

"I know. I just love America. Is great land of opportunity, yes?"

"For a select few perhaps, but for far too many others, well, they're not so lucky. The gap between the rich and poor is still real wide. I'm afraid that old American dream of rising from rags to riches overnight is pretty much a fairy tale and—"

The corners of Madalina's mouth had visibly dropped.

"I'm sorry," Woody said, jumping off his soapbox. "I didn't mean to lay anything heavy on you."

Growing up in a very liberal household, his reaction to politically sensitive subjects was always knee-jerk. But who was he to burst Madalina's bubble? It was normal for her to be pumped up about her newly adopted country. He felt like such an asshole. He needed to lighten up the conversation. Fast.

"So, ah, judging from your accent," said Woody, nervously chuckling, "I suspect you're not from ah, well, you know, Brooklyn."

Madalina cocked her head and furled her brow. "Excuse of me?"

"What I mean to say is, what country are you from?"

"Ah, from Romania."

He had this sudden urge to play connect the dots with every one of those freckles on her chest.

"I live on Black Sea. Is called Constanta. Very big city. Almost as big as Bucharest. Many touristic attractions. You must go sometime, I think."

"Who knows, perhaps I will. Maybe you can, you know, tell me more about your country sometime."

Woody bit his tongue. How could he have used such an unoriginal come-on line? He thought of himself as reasonably intelligent, but why was he acting like such a moron with this girl?

"It would be my pleasures to do this for you."

"You would?" he said, his voice cracking. Had she actually taken the bait and not regurgitated it? "I mean, of course, there's no rush and—"

"Oh, my God!" she exclaimed. "Look at time! I must go now or I will miss bus."

"I—I can give you a lift."

Had he been more confident, he would have offered to deliver Madalina right to her doorstep. Or clear across the continent if she asked.

"Thank you, Voody, is very kind for you."

"No big deal, really."

But it was, however, major to him. And as they walked along the path toward the parking lot, each strand of his overgrown mop of brown hair stood on end. Lucky he had on his trusty baseball cap.

"So what will you do tonight, Voody? You will go out to make party in South Beach, yes?"

"Oh, no," he said, tripping over a pebble on the pavement. "Not my thing. I'll go home. Grab some dinner. And then spend the rest of the evening working on the *Sponge*. The *Sea Sponge*. That's my sailboat. Or what will become my sailboat."

"How big is *Sea Sponge*?"

"Thirty-seven feet. Not small, but not a yacht."

"My papa, he makes ships."

Sheeps.

It took him a second, but then he realized what she'd meant.

"Many people do this in Constanta. My papa, he is, how you say? He work with fire."

"You mean a welder? Your dad uses a blow torch to melt the steel together?"

In order to help her understand, Woody tried pantomime. This spasticlike charade tickled Madalina.

"That was pretty lame, huh?"

"Elizabeth, she is right. You are so cute and sweet. I like you, Voody."

He angled the brim of his hat down another notch and kept walking straight ahead.

"Well, this is me," he said, patting the hood of a 1984 red pickup truck with numerous burnt-orange rust spots. "Not much to look at. A bit bent up, but the old gal gets me where I'm supposed to go. At least most of the time."

Woody opened the passenger door for her.

"You keep unlocked?" she asked.

"Of course. I mean, who'd want to steal this truck anyway," he said, laughing nervously.

Meanwhile, Woody discovered there was no room for Madalina to sit. He gathered a mound of papers, a cereal box, several empty coffee cups, a can of WD–40, a book on celestial navigation and a half-eaten piece of rawhide and in one fell swoop, dumped them all behind the seat.

"This is as good as it's going to get, I'm afraid," he said, giving the stained, torn upholstery a quick brush with the side of his hand, before heading to the driver's side.

"You have dog, yes?" asked Madalina.

"Guess the hair was a dead give-away," he said, sliding in next to her. "I've got this big old mutt who wandered into our yard one day when she was a pup. Name's Sweetie. Hands down, she's the love of my life. I mean, well, you know, in a manner of speaking she is," he said, laughing nervously. "So, ah, do you like dogs?"

"We had back in my country when I was girl. But dog is very dead now."

Woody offered his condolences, and then turned the key in the ignition only to discover his truck had suffered the same fate.

"What is wrong?"

"It's the battery."

"Is bad?"

"Well, it's not too good."

"Maybe I should start to make walk now, yes?"

But before Woody had a chance to convince Madalina to do otherwise, the artillery arrived.

A fully loaded H1 Alpha Hummer to be exact.

Bright "cock-blocking" yellow.

The left window of the Hummer opened. A burst of cold air along with the musical offerings of U2 blew out, followed by the appearance of a face with which Woody had been familiar for over ten years.

"Transportation problems, I presume?"

There was only one reason why an obnoxious prick like Hollings would skulk around someplace as "undesirable" as the employee's parking lot, and Woody knew it had nothing to do with roadside assistance.

"Hey, Madalina! Remember me from this afternoon?"

"You are Todd, yes?"

Madalina pronounced his name so it sounded more like "toad." A most appropriate choice, thought Woody.

"I came by the café to see if you needed a ride home," said Todd. "But they said you'd just left. Or at least tried to, that is. Seeing as the Woodmeister here isn't going anywhere anytime soon, looks like things have changed. Can I give you a lift?"

The girl's eyes scanned the Hummer and then back across the truck. It was obvious which vehicle she preferred.

"You're in a rush," said Woody. "It's all right. Go ahead with Todd."

Madalina smiled plaintively and hugged her shoulders. "But I feel so bad . . ."

"Don't worry. I'm cool."

But this was far from the case.

Woody, now plumb out of ammunition, had simply surrendered without a fight.

Chapter 2

Woody revved up his engine one last time.

"You all set, man," said Ariel, draping the jumper cables over his shoulder.

Ariel Vega, the club's prized mechanic, was a stocky, middle-aged Afro-Cuban with golden fingers and a heart to match. When he was fifteen, he, along with his mother and ten other Balseros, had struggled onto the Miami shore after spending several weeks on a vessel bearing no resemblance to a Carnival cruise ship. This determined immigrant now owned a piece of his own American Dream—a modest home in Little Havana with money reserved for his kids' college education; a privilege which he, himself, had been denied.

"What's the matter with you, man? You look lower than a snake's asshole."

"Don't wanna talk about it."

"This has something to do with that new waitress, don't it? Elizabeth said she could tell you got it bad for her. Maybe you get to do the horizontal cha-cha-cha with her?"

Ariel closed his eyes, pursed his mouth and gyrated his hips to demonstrate.

"Can we please leave my sex life out of this discussion? Besides, Madalina . . ."

"You should see how your eyes light up when you say her name. So what's her problemo? She playing hard to get or something? I can help you if you got a problem. Make you an ebo. No sweat."

Ariel, as did many of his island ancestors, practiced Santeria, a five-hundred-year-old religion imbuing African beliefs with Catholicism. An "ebo" was a spell which, among a multitude of uses, promised to remedy any number of physical, emotional or even financial maladies.

"Lemme give you a small stick of Jamaica rosewood. Next time you speak to her, you gotta chew it up and leave it in your mouth. I'm telling you, man, you do this and the girl will be yours."

"Appreciate the offer," said Woody. "But no thanks. I'm afraid it'd take a whole helluva lot of magic to ever get with a girl like that."

Traffic on US1 moved as fast as a becalmed sailboat in a sea of sludge. But then again, what with rampant construction and overpopulation, getting nowhere fast anywhere, anytime, in Miami was a sure thing.

About a mile from the club, Woody's air-conditioning crapped out. Opening the windows provided no relief from the heat and humidity, and within a few minutes he was a sweaty mess.

Needless to say, Woody was especially grateful to finally reach the turnoff for Rickenbacker Causeway. He left the gridlock behind and sped across Biscayne Bay, relishing the cross breezes which wicked the moisture from his body. It took him two minutes to traverse Virginia Key, and in the final leg of his commute, he ascended the mountainous William Powell Bridge which deposited him onto the barrier island he had called home since the age of five.

* * *

Shortly after his mother passed away, Woody and his father, Mike Woods, moved from a sleepy northwest corner of Connecticut to Key Biscayne where they had been invited to stay with Mike's older sister, Katherine, and her husband, Herb Arnold, until permanent housing was found.

Woody's aunt and uncle had purchased their modest, two-bedroom ranch on West Mashta Drive with its panoramic view of Biscayne Bay for thirty-five grand in the late fifties when the population of the Key consisted of World War II vets, stoned artists, assorted Bohemian types and battalions of kamikaze mosquitoes. In those days anyone who willingly chose to reside on this island, with its cookie-cutter Mackle houses and the village's one working pay phone, was considered nuts. Fast forward to the twenty-first century and Herb and Katherine Arnold's hurricane-battered, cement-walled box was now worth somewhere in the vicinity of eight million bucks. As a tear-down!

Meanwhile, Mike Woods, a freelance international photo journalist, accepted every extended assignment that came his way. Woody saw his dad so infrequently, the tot began to think of Katherine and Herb as his real parents and Mike as this Star Wars–type "action figure" who landed on earth every now and again armed with tales of heroism and wielding a light saber camouflaged as a banjo. Unfortunately, the "force" was not with Mike Woods when, less than a year later, a freak accident off the coast of Cyprus cost him his life and orphaned his son.

As his sole guardians, Woody's aunt and uncle embraced the opportunity to nurture the child they could never have on their own. Who cared that they were old enough to be his grandparents? They absolutely adored him.

Katherine taught science at a ritzy private school in Coconut Grove. Although neither she nor her husband, a professor of mechanical engineering at the University of Miami, were thrilled

to have Woody fraternize with those "rich, spoiled brats," the al-
lure of superior—and free—education at Grove Prep couldn't
be ignored.

Woody's love affair with the ocean began the day he arrived
in South Florida. Thanks especially to his uncle, who was a sailing nut. Herb had joined the Trade Winds Yacht Club back in
the days when a lifetime membership could be bought for
peanuts; and he had moored his boat, the *Lady Katherine,* there.
The irony was that his wife, after whom the thirty-foot sloop
was named, was prone to extreme seasickness and never once
went sailing. Not so with "the boys," who were on the water at
every opportunity.

It was also Herb who taught his young nephew how to
work with wood (giving additional meaning to his nickname).
From model ships to furniture, their crowning achievement was
a fourteen-foot wooden skiff which, along with the *Lady
Katherine,* was lost years later during Hurricane Andrew.

When it came time for college, Woody reluctantly accepted
a scholarship at the University of Iowa so he could, at Katherine's
suggestion, "get a taste of middle America" while taking advan-
tage of a top-notch writing program. But the land-locked campus
made Woody claustrophobic and terribly homesick. He finished
out his freshman year and then transferred to the University of
Miami which, like Grove Prep, was tuition-free for the kin of
tenured professors.

Upon graduation, Woody, like many Gen-Xers, moved back
in with his aunt and uncle until he figured out what to do with
the rest of his life. Sure, he loved the creative word, but aside
from one published short story in a quirky periodical, the starving-
writer route was not financially viable.

Straight journalism wasn't exactly his bag. At least at the
entry level. Besides, he'd most likely have to relocate to some
obscure town to report for an obscure paper for however long it
took until he broke out of, well, obscurity.

Graduate school didn't appeal. Much to the chagrin of his erudite guardians, Woody had no interest in teaching anything other than sailing. And forget about a law degree. His aunt and uncle often compared attorneys to subhumans who performed unthinkable acts with puppies.

In the interim, Woody fell back on his old job at the Trade Winds Yacht Club where he had worked summers and holidays since the seventh grade. And when Skip Edwards offered Woody the newly vacant position of assistant dockmaster, he readily accepted the job as an in-between until something more suitable came along.

Who could have guessed, after six years, he'd still be there?

Unfortunately, that same summer after his college graduation, Herb Arnold was diagnosed with prostate cancer. While he was in the hospital, his nephew read to him from one of their favorite books—about a captain named Joshua Slocum who, at the turn of the nineteenth century, rebuilt a wooden mess of a tub named the *Spray* and single-handedly sailed the thirty-six-foot boat around the world. Slocum's memoir of his travels—*Sailing Alone Around the World*—became a best-selling seafaring classic.

With Herb's enthusiastic endorsement, a seed was thus planted in his nephew's brain. The realization of which would take a lot more time, effort and money than anyone could have ever imagined. Nonetheless, fueled by the memory of his uncle, who died that same year, Woody maintained a steady course to fulfilling his dream.

From the air, Key Biscayne—originally claimed by Ponce de Leon for Spain in 1515—looks rather like a vegetative sandwich. Two state parks—Crandon on the north and Bill Baggs on the south—flank the four-mile long island, and squeezed in the middle, from the bay to the ocean side, are single-family homes and high-density condo developments. To some, this "arrangement" might be interpreted as Mother Nature's way of containing urban sprawl. But to others, an impediment to "twenty-first century progress."

Woody followed the island's sole access road—lined with nothing but subtropical flora for the first two miles—into the village of Key Biscayne. Far from sleepy, this micro-mini metropolis consists of several two-story, tastefully constructed strip malls, a gas station, a smattering of restaurants, a large Winn Dixie supermarket, a community center, a village green and a snazzy new firehouse. This being high season, Crandon Boulevard swayed under the weight of the combined bank accounts of its part-time residents, many for whom English was not their first language.

But despite how much the island's profile had changed in the twenty-three years he'd lived there, the simple home Woody shared with his now widowed aunt Katherine remained constant.

Two cars were parked in the gravel driveway of 42 West Mashta Drive. Katherine Arnold's ancient white Datsun—covered with politically charged bumper stickers—and her best friend Dorothy Little's silver Cadillac with its silly "Dot2Trot" vanity plate.

Woody pulled up on the grass next to a mastless hull which, after over four and a half years of defying hurricane season, was still firmly balanced on jack stands. He took a moment to admire the keel of the *Sea Sponge*, which he'd painted with red lead preservative early that morning, but when he heard his mutt, Sweetie, barking, he hustled along to the house.

The moment Woody walked through the front door, the sixty-pound lapdog jumped into her beloved's arms and slathered his face with her flat noodle of a tongue. He found her breath particularly atrocious.

"What on earth have you gotten into?"

Sweetie looked at him as if to say, *Beats the shit outta me.*
Which basically meant, *I love you but why bother asking me a question I can never answer?*

"That you, Woody?" called a gravelly female voice from the kitchen.

"You were expecting Donald Trump, perhaps?"

"Very funny!" came the response. "Now, you and your wise ass better hightail it in here and give your old aunt some sugar."

Before he took another step, however, Woody dutifully removed his Top-Siders. Katherine had had this no-shoes rule ever since he could remember. Judging from the massive amount of clutter everywhere, she certainly wasn't anal. Nor was this New Orleans–born woman of Japanese descent. She had simply decided to adopt this centuries-old custom of "leaving the outside world, outside" in order to provide a "sanctuary where one's bare feet can breathe in a dirt-free environment."

Katherine Arnold also had a very definite opinion about interior design. In the main living area there were cerulean blue walls and curtains. Shelves crammed with coral, starfish and shells of every size. A coffee table made of driftwood, another from lobster traps. Sconces fashioned from conches. Lamp bases made out of pieces of polished sea glass. A thirty-gallon salt-water fish tank. Paintings of beach sunsets and rolling waves. And finally on the floor, sand-colored shag carpeting. Call it aquatic overkill, but Woody, whose whole life revolved around the ocean, rather dug it.

Woody found his Aunt seated at the ship's wheel kitchen table he and Uncle Herb had built for her many years back. Petite and trim, save for her kangaroo-pouch middle, three-quarters of her body was all legs. She wore her white hair plaited into her signature braids, and her face—thanks to avoiding the sun, and genes—looked more than a decade younger than her seventy-nine years. A quirky dresser, today Katherine had on purple leggings and one of her favorite T-shirts, which depicted a red-cheeked blowfish and the tagline, *Puffed up about the environment.*

To Katherine's left sat her buddy, Dorothy, a former cabaret singer with big hair, big heart and a big appetite for everything from food to politics. Dorothy had lost her husband a year prior to moving to a condo on the Key.

Now, given that Katherine served on the steering committees of several local activist groups—among them, the Sierra Club and the Audubon Society—it was not unusual to see any number of ladies—mostly widows over the age of sixty-five—gathered at the house. But today somebody from a different demographic had joined the group. Specifically, a girl in her early twenties.

If called to describe one feature of her face, however, Woody would have been at a loss. He'd become visually impaired ever since laying eyes on a certain Romanian waitress.

"Hey, ladies," he said.

He walked up to his aunt, leaned over and kissed her forehead. She was always a bit warm to the touch.

"Woody, honey," said Dorothy. "I'd like to introduce you to my Kristin."

She had pestered him about meeting her granddaughter the few times she'd visited from up north, but he had always created some emergency that needed attention. This time, however, Dorothy had obviously pulled a fast one on him.

"Oh, well, nice to, ah, meet you."

It was against his nature to be rude.

The girl, in turn, mumbled an unenthusiastic salutation and resumed stuffing envelopes. Seemed she had been the victim of a setup as well and was none too pleased.

"Kristin's staying with me for a month," said Dorothy. "She's going to work on that Everglades restoration project. I told you she's getting a master's degree in environmental studies at Brown, didn't I? She's also an excellent sailor and just so happens to have broken up with her boyfriend and—"

"Grandma," she groaned. "No offense, but could you please cut the sales pitch?"

Woody chuckled to himself. Only hours ago, he'd used the same line with Elizabeth.

Back there at the Spinnaker Café.

Standing next to Madalina.

He could still smell her hair.

Hear her giggle.

Feel the way her tiny fingers slowly slid across the palm of his hand.

Woody suddenly felt a stirring in his boxers.

"Man, am I ever thirsty!"

And with that, he leapt in front of the refrigerator. Flinging open the door, he discretely brushed the front of his pants and confirmed the diagnosis. His only option was to pretend to rummage through the shelves until the cold air, hopefully, remedied the situation.

"We out of chocolate milk?"

"Just bought a new carton," said Katherine. "It's between my prune juice and flaxseed oil."

Woody reached for the container and was about to close the fridge when he zeroed in on a large stainless steel bowl filled with cookie batter. He was about to steal a golf-sized ball of the dough which Katherine always let "season" prior to baking, when she interceded.

"I know what you're up to! Get your dirty mitts out of there!"

"Aw, come on, just a little taste. Just to make sure it's not poisonous."

"Poisonous, eh?" asked Dorothy, laughing.

"Would you believe he's been giving me the same bullshit line since he was six?"

"Yeah," said Woody, pouring himself a large glass of chocolate milk and downing it in one gulp. "And she's been falling for it just as long."

Bloody Mary in hand, Katherine followed her nephew outside to the flagstone backyard patio.

"Ought to be a good one tonight," she said, pulling up a chipped cast-iron chair. "No haze, clearly delineated horizon."

Back when Herb was alive, the three of them would often gather to watch the "best free show in the world"—namely an unobstructed view of the sun setting over Biscayne Bay. Nowadays, the only way she could capture Woody's attention long enough was to assign him grill duty.

"Too bad Dorothy and her granddaughter couldn't stay for dinner."

"Yeah, what a pity," said Woody, throwing back a bottle of beer.

"Don't be a wiseass. You know, it might be good for you to get out a little."

Woody stoked the fire and didn't respond.

Katherine stared at the boy. His face was nearly a carbon copy of her late brother's. The angular profile. Those full lips. Those large, deep hazel eyes. Same nose. Same hairline. Minus that ragged scar on Mike's chin for which Katherine felt responsible when she, at age fifteen, had briefly turned her back on her baby brother.

"Kristin seems like such a nice girl. And so smart. You two certainly have common interests."

"Please don't meddle," said Woody. "You know I've got no time."

Katherine had promised herself never to intercede with her nephew's future plans. Still, every once in a while she was guilty of subliminal persuasion. Who could blame her for wishing Woody might have a change of heart and stay close to home.

"But I just thought it might be good for you to get out a little, Clarence. Have a little fun."

"Oh, boy," he said, moaning. "Playing the formal-name card. This is major. Look, I'm doing fine doing what I'm doing."

"But you look exhausted."

"It's just been a long day."

"Well, then, sugar, why don't you give yourself a rest tonight? There's all day tomorrow to work on the boat and—"

"Not exactly," said Woody, interrupting. "I got offered this private teaching gig."

"A kid?"

"No."

"One of those horny married women?"

"Give me a break."

"Why are you being so mysterious, then?"

"I'm not. He's a new member. Guy bought a forty-five-foot stinkpot he's got no idea how to handle."

"Sounds like a real asshole. You think it'll be worth the aggravation?"

"For three hundred bucks I think I can—"

Woody jumped out of his seat.

"Holy shit," he cried, pointing at the horizon. "Look at that!"

"Look at what?"

"Shit, it's gone. It was a burst of green light over the water! Just near the top edge of the sun."

Katherine gripped the sides of the chair and leaned forward. "You mean to tell me you just saw a green flash?"

She had taught Woody about this phenomenon many years ago. A "green flash" could be witnessed only at dawn or dusk when atmospheric refraction was at its max. Neither she nor Herb had ever seen one. The only person she knew who claimed he had was one Captain Jimmy O'Neil, a longtime native who ran a charter fishing boat out of Key Biscayne. The "flash" he claimed to have seen was off the coast of Cuba. When he was, no doubt, drunk as a skunk.

"It was more like a green dot rather than a flash and lasted just a second or two," said Woody. "But I'm telling you, this was the real deal."

"Well, then, sugar," said Katherine. "Count yourself as one lucky guy."

Chapter 3

Todd parked his Hummer next to his dad's Ferrari which sat a safe distance away from his mother's Jaguar convertible and the family's Porsche SUV. The only vehicle missing was that of his sister, Carolina. In one year, two months and eleven days, she'd earn her driver's license. Todd wondered what kind of car his father would buy that spoiled metal-mouthed velociraptor.

He found his parents sitting outside by the pool. His mother, Ashley, struggled to maneuver her artificially enhanced lips into something vaguely resembling a smile. The end effect, as far as Todd was concerned, made her look rather like a chimpanzee.

"My baby boy!" she exclaimed, bounding toward him with open arms.

"Whoa, Ma, take it easy."

In some circles, his mother's new rack could be mistaken for a dangerous weapon.

His father was busy talking on the phone. Avoiding eye contact, Stanford Hollings acknowledged his son's appearance by a dismissive tilt of his palm.

With some ten thousand luxury condos under his and his partners' belts, this former ambulance-chasing attorney (born Stanley Holacheck from the Bronx) had done very well for himself. Todd aspired to be like his dad—minus the hair-plugs, dye job and double chin, of course—mainly because in South Florida, people likened highly successful real estate developers to rock stars.

"Tomorrow night's free, right, Ashley?" Stanford asked his wife.

"Actually no, dear. We've got that Sierra Club benefit."

"Just what I need—environmental terrorists in black tie."

"But I thought you said it was good public relations to keep them out of your hair," she said.

"They got our money already, so who cares? We're going to have dinner with Carlos Lagosto about a possible deal."

"But I just bought a new Michael Kors gown and—"

"Forget about it," Stanford snapped. "You've been overruled and the case is closed."

Everyone on the payroll—family and employees alike—knew that once a Hollings verdict had been reached, the case was closed with no chance for appeal.

"Well, I suppose I could wear the gown at that Republican fund-raiser we've got next month," mumbled Ashley to deaf ears.

Todd sat down on a chaise lounge next to his father.

"So what's up, Pops?"

"What's up? I'll tell you what's up. I heard you were a no-show at the site yesterday."

"But it was Saturday . . ."

"I don't give a shit. It's still a work day. I intend for you, as my representative, to make an appearance whenever and wherever I tell you to."

"But—"

"No buts. If you think you can waltz right up the corporate ladder without working your ass off, well, here's a major news flash for you, sonny boy. Forget about it."

"You're being a bit harsh, Stanford," said Ashley. "Go easy on my baby boy."

"Did you ever consider the notion that if you'd stop treating him as an infant, your so-called baby boy might become more responsible?"

"Hey, hold on," said Todd. "I graduated from college."

"By the skin of your straightened and bleached teeth."

"I've got my own apartment."

"That I purchased. In a building that I own."

"Jesus, I have a job."

"A job at MY company! A position which, at any moment, could be terminated. I don't want anybody talking behind my back about the boss's son slacking off and spending more time cruising the Web for porn than he does trying to hustle up business. I've got plenty of other kids who may not have had an Ivy League education like yours, but are willing to put in the hours to make their mark."

"Hey, that's not exactly fair, Dad. I'm getting real close on that deal with Gustavo Tinnie."

"Oh, yeah? Well, I'll tell you what." Stanford Hollings positioned his face right in his son's. "You convince that old fart to sell his property and we might just be talking about a whole new ball game."

Chapter 4

Barring illness or bad weather, no day passed that Woody failed to work on his boat. For a guy who had avoided commitment since losing his virginity in the eleventh grade, this was the one relationship to which he could commit. He'd never desert the *Sea Sponge,* and he knew as long as she stayed afloat, she'd always be there for him. In good weather she would be his lover, and in a storm she would be his mother, protecting him to the best of her ability.

The *Sea Sponge* had been owned by Spencer Cabot, one of the founding members of the Trade Winds Yacht Club, who sadly had spent the last quarter of his one hundred years confined to a wheelchair. Cabot's sailboat, a thirty-seven foot wooden, double-ended gaff cutter, was built in 1948 in the style of the famed Norwegian nautical architects, Colin and Archer, and had been sitting "on the hard" for a half decade while his heirs fought over his rather sizeable estate.

By the time Woody found her, the *Sea Sponge* was in pretty bad shape. Extensive dry rot and years of assault and battery by the elements had rendered her unseaworthy, so the only way to transport the *Sponge* from Coconut Grove to Key Biscayne was to haul her across land. Before Woody had lifted a finger, the cost of the boat plus moving expenses had emptied his savings account of ten thousand dollars. On a good day, he preferred to think it was a small price to pay for love. But on a bad one, he'd ruminate about the grip the *Sponge* had on him—emotionally, financially and physically.

As all veteran wooden boat enthusiasts knew, "In order to get to the bad it's necessary to destroy just about everything good." This, translated, meant stripping the *Sea Sponge* down to its shell. The frame completely replanked with hard pine. The teak deck salvaged, refinished and caulked. Every bronze fastener—the two thousand or more pegs that held the entire boat together—pulled and substituted with new ones. Plumbing and electrical updated, including the engine which Woody bought secondhand, of course. He rebuilt the deckhouse—from the sole to the ceiling—from scratch. And now with approximately eight months out from dropping her into the water, Woody was frantically installing cabinetry and framing out his sleeping quarters.

After dinner, as was his routine, Woody and Sweetie headed for the *Sea Sponge*. Hoisting his dog on his shoulder, he climbed up the ladder. The focus of tonight's project was to put the finishing touches on the forward berth, but a half hour in, it was obvious he just wasn't into it.

Madalina.

Try as he might, he couldn't get her out of his mind, reviewing every moment shared with her. The good and the embarrassingly horrendous.

No sooner had Woody concluded that all things considered it was safer to steer clear of any female entanglements, than a mosquito, thrown off course by the glare of several pot-lights, decided to use his right eyebrow as a landing strip. With his one free hand, Woody attempted to smash the wayward aviator, but missed.

In a second attempt, he miscalculated the amount of space between his head and the ceiling and knocked himself out cold.

The mosquito, however, lived to tell the tale.

Chapter 5

Woody readjusted his mask and was about to continue his descent when he heard a dog bark. Naturally, at six fathoms beneath the surface of the ocean, this gave him pause.

As did the mouthful of teeth that had just clamped down on his bicep.

Was it a shark?

A moray eel?

Given the circumstances, Woody figured it might be time to blow out of this potential nightmare in the works. He forced open his right eye and discovered his dog's snout right in his face.

"Whew. Am I happy to see you, girl!"

The pooch responded in kind by drenching her master with sloppy kisses. Woody started to slough off the saliva from his face when he felt a very tender knot in the upper right corner of his forehead and realized he was not tucked under the bedcovers, but sprawled on top of a bare wooden slab.

The moment Woody walked through the back door of the house, he could smell Katherine's French-pressed hazelnut coffee and hear CNN blasting in the kitchen.

Woody shouted a "good morning" to Katherine and made a beeline for the bathroom. He shut the door and peered into the vanity mirror. The welt, raised with shades of blue, was as noticeable as it was sore. Unfortunately, concealing his injury under his baseball cap—an item he never left home without—would not be an option today. The brim was too tight.

He removed his clothes and stepped into the shower. Given the poor water pressure, the spray did little to alleviate his stiff back. Then he cut his chin in several places while shaving. With tissue paper affixed to his nicks, he dressed and, against his better judgment, headed for the kitchen.

"Good morning," he said, sneaking around the back of Katherine's chair.

"Morning, sugar," she said. "Sleep well?"

"Ah, yeah. Just like a log."

In more ways than one, he thought.

"Can I get you some oatmeal?"

Woody often threatened to use a pot of Katherine's favorite breakfast cereal to caulk his boat.

"Not in this lifetime."

He poured himself a cup of black coffee and filled an enormous bowl with equal portions of Cheerios, Captain Crunch, Golden Grahams and some of Katherine's homemade granola.

"Come sit down at the table like a civilized person."

"But I'm in a rush," he said, fully intending to eat his cereal at the counter and run.

Katherine didn't buy this excuse and suddenly appeared at his side.

"What the HELL did you do to yourself?"

"Nothing. It's fine, seriously."

"Bullshit. That's quite a nasty bump."

Woody tried not to wince while she probed it with her fingers.

"We should have this looked at."

"No way. Completely unnecessary."

"Maybe you need an X ray or an MRI?"

"Aunt Katherine, please."

"You did this last night on the boat, didn't you?"

"Yeah, so. Comes with the territory. You ought to know this by now."

"With all that dangerous stuff lying around, it's a wonder you haven't been really hurt and—"

"Listen," said Woody, interrupting. "What's going to happen when I'm alone at sea and I get a scratch? Are you going to helicopter over with a Band–Aid?"

"Don't be a wiseass to your old auntie."

"Sorry, but seriously, let's drop the histrionics. I promise you, I'm fully capable of taking care of myself."

Katherine opened her mouth to protest and then decided to leave her nephew alone.

Provided he agreed to sit down at the table to finish his breakfast.

"Look what I got, Freddy," said Trish, pulling a bottle of Dom Perignon out of her *Hermès* bag.

"Isn't it a little early for hooch?"

"No, silly. We need to christen your new boat. I saw someone do this in a movie. I think it was *Titanic* or something."

After giving Fred the cold shoulder last night, was it possible that Trish had decided to sanction this extravagant indulgence?

Or did she have an ulterior motive?

Although Fred figured the latter was probably the case, he concluded he really didn't give a shit if it cost him a bundle. After all, he did have the privilege of slipping into that luscious body of hers every night.

Trish—in gold flip-flops and a low-cut, white micro-mini dress—climbed aboard the vessel. Fred followed close behind, trying to appear as confident as his fiancée.

"Well, here goes," said Trish. "I'm so excited!"

She leaned over the port side, her breasts nearly falling out of her scoop neck.

"I christen thee the *Midas Touch*!"

She cracked the champagne across the fiberglass, but the bottle remained intact. A second attempt proved equally unsuccessful.

"I lift weights," she whined. "Why won't it fucking break already?"

"It's more about the angle of the dangle," said Fred. "Let me give it a try."

One swift wack to the corner of the stern did the trick. Trish and Fred applauded, clearly oblivious to the nicks the hull had sustained during the christening ceremony.

"So what's my delicious honey bunny up to today?"

"I'm meeting Carla for breakfast at Big Pink, and then I have my trainer. After that I may do a little shopping."

"Baby, since when do you ever do a 'little' shopping?"

"I thought I'd get some new lingerie."

Fred grinned like a Cheshire cat. "Well, in that case. Buy out the whole damn place."

"Let's just hope you feel that way when you get your credit card bill," said Trish, giggling.

"But you're worth it, baby."

"Damn straight I am."

"Meet me back here at the club around four?"

"Yep. We'll celebrate."

"Celebrate what?"

"The fish you catch, natch."

Trish grabbed Fred's shirt and pulled him close to her chest. It really turned him on when she was so seductively aggressive.

"The really, really, really BIG fish you catch for me."

"I'll do my best, honey bunny," said Fred. "I'll do my best."

★　★　★

Guiding the *Midas Touch* safely out of its slip went better than expected until Fred nearly ran the boat aground coming through Dinner Key.

"Whoa, close call, huh?"

"There's little room for mistakes in this channel," said Woody, who'd grabbed the wheel in time and avoided disaster. "But take comfort in the fact that a former commodore of the club once ended up in the muck. Even after all these years, dude's still referred to as 'Shipwreck Pete.'"

"Well, I intend to take this boating shit seriously."

"You certainly have the right attitude, Mr. Sage."

"Fred. Please, call me Fred."

Anyway, Fred's enthusiasm began to plummet about a mile off Coconut Grove. Queasiness was followed by extreme nausea, and by the time they made it to the open ocean, Woody's student was in bad shape.

First, Fred purged himself of breakfast: a Western omelet, home fries, extra bacon and Trish's half-eaten chocolate chip waffle. Then he expelled his oysters Rockefeller, Chateaubriand, duchess potatoes and crème brûlée from the night before.

"I'm going to turn the boat around and head back," shouted Woody from the flying bridge where he was thankfully well out of the line of fire.

"Don't you dare!" insisted Fred, now the color of Kentucky bluegrass. "Trust me, I'll get through this. I'm one tough motherfucker."

"Are you sure about this?"

"Absolutely. How much more could I possibly puke anyway? I'm going to go below, grab me a couple Dramamines, and then we'll go catch us a fish."

Obeying the "captain's" orders, Woody pushed the throttle forward and opened up the diesel engines. But when Fred neglected to reappear after about a half hour, Woody was concerned.

Idling the engine, he shifted into neutral and then went to investigate.

There was no sign of him in the cockpit. Nor in the salon or the head. He did, however, find Fred in the master stateroom. Spread-eagled across the king-sized bed.

Woody gently nudged Fred. He, in turn, babbled something about Madonna cooking him sausage and peppers while singing "Material Girl."

Nude.

In the lotus position.

Or at least that was what it sounded like he'd said.

"Exactly how many of those pills did you take?"

"About two. No three. Or maybe five."

Which certainly explains the strange, hallucinatory behavior, thought Woody. "This isn't good," he said. "I need to get you back to the club."

"No, no, we can't do that!"

Fred grabbed hold of Woody's arm with the strength of a newborn. "I promised Trish. Please don't take me back. I'll throw in an extra two hundred and fifty clams if you catch a, a . . ."

"Fish?" suggested Woody.

"Precisely. Bigger the better. I'm trusting you, bro. Don't let me down."

And with that, Fred Sage, erstwhile conqueror of the seven seas, fell fast asleep on the job.

Woody settled into one of the two fighting chairs bolted to the cockpit floor and inserted the end of a nine-foot fishing rod into the holder cup positioned between his thighs. He had every intention to focus on his mission, but within minutes began to fidget as if seated on barbed wire. Not only did he lack the patience or aptitude for fishing, but the sport was far too inactive for him.

The reluctant angler stared out at the ocean. Flat, save for a few ripples, there were no boats in sight. No birds. And, alas, with the exception of the sardine he'd used as bait, no sign of any fish.

Spending time on the water always made Woody even more ravenous than he was on land. If that was at all possible. Good thing the boy was blessed with a supercharged metabolism. His host had graciously provided him with an Italian cold cut hero, chips, honey mustard pretzels and a Blondie, all of which he promptly devoured. He washed it all down with a bottle of water, belched and then took a leak off the side of the boat.

Meanwhile, almost thirty minutes had passed and still not a bite on his line . . .

Woody finished the last chapters of Rudyard Kipling's *Captains Courageous*, enjoying it as much as he did when he'd read the classic as a teen.

Another hour passed and not as much as a nibble . . .

He flipped through his latest issue of *WoodenBoat Magazine*. An article on the Hardanger Fartøyvernsenter, a famous Norwegian wooden boat restoration center, intrigued him, and he made a mental note to visit the place someday.

Twenty-three minutes whizzed by. Tick-tock.

Next, he reached for his banjo. As his schedule allowed little time for practice, he'd brought it along just in case there was any down time. This five-stringed Deering—handmade in California over thirty years ago—had belonged to his dad and was one of Woody's most prized possessions. Plastered with frayed stickers from the elder Woods's global travels, the carrying case was in sad shape, but Woody could never bring himself to update it.

As for the banjo, well, thanks to Woody's loving care, the instrument was like new. Its carved mahogany neck and resonator had been finished with a satinlike lacquer. Hearts and flowers were etched into its Brazilian rosewood fretboard along with mother-of-pearl inlays. Certainly a beauty to behold for those in the know.

A self-taught musician of less than remarkable merit, Woody

could fake some bluegrass; his favorite (as well as his father's) being a much slower rendition of an Earl Scrugg's classic known as the "Foggy Mountain Breakdown." He slipped a plastic pick on his thumb and two metal fingerpicks on his other fingers, and began to play this very tune. Several bars in, his tackle began to twitch.

It's probably nothing, he thought and kept playing until the fishing pole suddenly bent over so far he feared it'd snap in two. He must have hooked something of significance. Hopefully, not an underwater cable.

Woody quickly stowed away his banjo, grabbed hold of the rod with both hands and began to crank the reel with a vengeance. The battle took much longer than expected. But finally, he saw a fish jump out of the water, about fifteen feet off the stern.

The creature was deep purplish in color with a spined dorsal fin crowning the top of its back. Its belly and sides were silvery, and a bunch of dark hyphenated lines ran the length of its body. Woody guessed the fish to be about forty pounds. Hard to believe, given the fight the little sucker put up.

He grabbed an aluminum gaff hook and climbed onto the fishing platform.

"Guess who's coming for dinner!" he proudly declared out loud.

"YOUR WORST NIGHTMARE IF YOU DON'T SET ME FREE!"

The voice was deep, slightly nasal and peppered with what sounded like a heavy Brooklyn accent.

"Fred?" shouted Woody, surveying the area.

Mr. Sage, however, was still missing in action.

"Shit, my mind must be playing tricks on me."

Woody leaned over to haul aboard the fish, but to his surprise it spit him right in the eye!

"WHATZAMATTER WITH YOU? DON'T YOU UNDERSTAND ENGLISH? I SAID, LEMME GO!"

Woody screamed, slipped and nearly did a back flip into the drink!

"GUESS I GOT YOUR ATTENTION NOW, HUH, ASS-HOLE?"

"Please tell me you didn't, ah, actually, I mean, did you just say something to me?"

"Well, it sure as shit wasn't Howard Stern!"

Woody stared at the fish.

"Look, kid, there's been a serious mix-up here. So maybe I failed to read the small print, but I can tell ya, getting caught was definitely not in MY contract."

Sure enough. The fish moved his mouth—lined with small, conical teeth—with each word he spoke.

"This can't be possible," muttered Woody. "I must have gotten too much sun. Yeah, that's what it is. Or maybe Katherine was right. Maybe I do have a concussion."

"Will ya do us both a favor here, kid? Cut the babbling and set me free already. I don't have all day here, you know. Time is money. Especially in this town."

"Listen, you! You're, you're just a figment of my imagination and this conversation is officially o-v-e-r!"

"But think about what you're about to do, kid."

"Trust me, I am."

"You want to land in a shrink's office every Tuesday afternoon until you kick the bucket? Because I'm telling you, that's what'll happen if you take the life of an innocent man like me."

"Excuse me. But did you just refer to yourself as a 'man'?"

"Minor detail."

"Ha! Funny. Joke, right?"

"Will you at least hear me out first?"

"Why, do you have something of huge intellectual importance to report? Or do you just want to share a recipe for chocolate cake?"

"With all the fishermen in the sea, I gotta get caught by a wiseass."

"Shit happens," said Woody. And this was a mountain's worth!

"Look, kid, how about we start this all over again?"

Woody rubbed his head. "Why would we possibly want to do that?"

The fish cleared his throat and fluttered his right fin. All so very proper.

"Allow me to introduce myself. Name's Raymond Prince. But everybody calls me the Prince."

"Because you're next in line for the British throne or something?"

"Come on, stay with me here. What's your name, kid?"

"Clarence Woods. But you can call me Woody."

"Why, because you keep sprouting them?"

The fish's laugh reminded Woody of someone gargling with epoxy.

"Not funny. If I were you, Your Royal Highness, I sure as hell wouldn't quit my day job."

"Due to circumstances beyond my control, seems to me I already have."

And with that, the fish began to wail. "Whether or not you may believe this, I used to have the whole five-star enchilada. Looks like George Clooney. A slew of car dealerships. A wife. Two beautiful grown daughters. Huge house on Alton Road, right on the Intercoastal. Big pool, Jacuzzi. Every electronic toy imaginable. But . . ."

"But what?"

"I always had a hard time keeping little Ray in my pants."

Woody refused to acknowledge what he thought he'd just heard.

"Get it? HARD time? Little Ray? Well, maybe not that little . . ."

"This is way too much information!"

"Whatever. Anyway, seems my old lady, well, the broad was highly connected."

"Connected?"

"Yeah, came from a long line of Italian witches."

"This just keeps getting weirder and weirder," Woody mumbled to himself.

"Anyway, one night I was closing a deal with this redhead. You should have seen the tits on this one! She'd come into the showroom dead set on a Honda Civic, but after dinner and several martinis, I had her convinced the Mercedes was the perfect match given the color of her eyes. If you get my gist."

"Not really, but do continue."

"Anyway, my wife, Sandy, well, her world completely revolved around our kids. Never seemed to care where I was or when I came home. Then the girls go off to college, and suddenly the broad has far too much free time. I bought her a rabbit to keep her company, but all of a sudden, Sandy decides she needs more."

"Hold on," interrupted Woody. "I'm totally lost in Wonderland here. Your wife had relations with a rabbit?"

"What hole have you been buried in? The Rabbit is the Rolls Royce of vibrators."

Woody massaged his temples. "Now I've heard everything."

"Anyway," the Prince continued. "Sandy catches me canoodling with the redhead and totally flips out. Next thing I know, poof, she does this mumbo-jumbo shtick and my life as I used to know it is gone in a flash. Me, Raymond Prince, stripped of my Armani suits and covered in scales. Me, a guy who hated crowds, schooling with hundreds of fucking fish! Me, a guy who never even learned how to dog paddle, never even dipped more than my ankles in the pool, swimming in the ocean, twenty-four-fucking-seven!"

"Whoa," said Woody. "That's pretty intense."

"You're telling me? But wait. Wait. It gets better. Here's the piece-dollar-resistance. Me, Raymond Prince, a strictly meat-

and-potatoes guy, a guy who couldn't even stomach the smell of seafood without feeling like he'd puke, gets transformed into the one food group he'd never be caught dead eating!"

"Seems you got the ultimate bait and switch, huh?"

"Not nice, kid. Not nice."

"Sorry, couldn't resist. So, ah, if you don't mind my asking, exactly what kind of fish did your wife turn you into?"

"I'll give you a hint. The kind that people like to mash up with mayo and throw between two slices of Wonder Bread."

"Tuna?"

"Kid's a genius! A skipjack tuna, to be exact. Otherwise known in some circles as a skipjack bonito, a mushmouth, skipper, skippy, striped tunny, victor fish, watermelon or a banjo."

"A banjo? That's pretty ironic, considering I happened to be playing my Deering when you grabbed my bait."

"I know. Always loved that theme from *Bonnie and Clyde*. Never mind how much I wanted to bang Faye Dunaway when I was a kid. You're obviously a very talented musician."

"Wouldn't go that far, but thanks, for the thumbs-up and all. It took me forever to learn the damn song."

"See, now you have to let me go. I mean, how could you knock off your biggest fan?"

Woody started to laugh. "Guess I just waltzed right into that trap, didn't I?"

"Well, that makes two of us, huh?"

"Okay, let's just say what you told me is true. How do you reverse this curse?"

The fish hesitated a moment. "It's kind of complicated, but I will tell you this. If I don't do what I've got to by the next full moon, the Prince here will be royally screwed."

"Why can't you tell me what it is? I mean, maybe there's something I can do to help and—"

"Ah-ha," interrupted Raymond. "Got the sympathy vote already. I'm so damn good."

"Huh?"

"You've got that gleam in your eye."

"What the hell are you talking about?"

"Your eyes—they're telling me a deal is about to be closed."

"Seeing as your car inventory is, ah, you know, nonexistent, I assume you're referring to your freedom."

"There is hope for the future generations of America!"

"But you see, I have a problem. The guy who owns this boat is depending on me to catch him a fish. In fact, he promised me a big tip if I do."

"Where is this schmuck anyway?"

"Seasick and passed out in the cabin."

"Captain Fucking Ahab!"

"Dude wanted to impress his fiancée."

"Typical. Pay someone else to do your dirty work so you can take the credit and get laid. Come to think of it, sounds like my kind of guy."

"You two actually remind me of each other," mumbled Woody.

"What'd you say?"

"It's not important."

"Everything you say is important, kid."

"Enough with the smooth talking. It's not necessary . . ."

The way Woody figured, he was either delusional or having another one of his wacko dreams, so what did anything matter anyway?

". . . I have every intention of letting you go."

"You are? You will? Oh, thank you! Thank you! What can the Prince do for you? You want a reward? I can get you plenty of cash. You want a fish? I'll give you a boatload. Anything you want, kid, anything. I'll make you a deal you won't forget. All you gotta do is ask."

"Don't worry, it's not important," said Woody as he turned

to leave. "Consider this act of kindness on the house. So good-bye, adieu, adios, see ya. It's been real."

"Wait!"

"Now what?"

"It's about this hook in my mouth. Kinda cramps the Prince's style, don't you think?"

Woody apologized for the oversight.

"I'll be right back. So, ah, you know, don't go anywhere."

"Always a comedian, this one is," cracked the fish.

Woody climbed back into the cockpit and found a pair of pliers in the tackle box.

"Now open wide," he said as he began to fumble around in the Prince's mouth.

"Hey, watch it, bubba! That hurts! This is a living, breathing creature you're dealing with here. Who the hell do you think you are? The Marquis de Sade?"

"Relax, I'm almost done."

Using the tool, Woody straightened out the curved wire of the hook. Then he slid his hand down the leader and, grasping it between his thumb and forefinger, yanked.

"There, you're—"

"FREE!"

Jubilant, the fish leapt high in the air and cannonballed into the water. Woody tried to avoid the back splash, but wasn't very successful.

"Just remember, kid, if you ever need anything, and I mean anything, all you have to do is ask."

Woody rolled his eyes. "And, ah, how exactly am I supposed to reach you? I don't remember getting a phone number or an e-mail address?"

"It's simple, wiseass," said Raymond as his body began to slowly descend below the surface of the water. "Simply play 'Foggy Mountain' on your banjo and the Prince will be at your beck and call."

Chapter 6

Woody intended to have Fred stationed at the steering wheel of the *Midas Touch* when they reentered the channel, but the man refused to cooperate. He was too busy serenading the pillow he'd wedged between his legs. A pillow he also appeared to be dry humping. Two notes in and it was clear Fred was not only tone-deaf, but could make Pavarotti sound like a cat in heat.

The good news was the *Midas Touch* had returned to the club unscathed. The bad was that the future Mrs. Sage was waiting at the dock. Along with two overstuffed shopping bags from Neiman Marcus and another from Prada.

"Where's my fiancé?"

"Well . . . ah . . . how can I put this?"

Before Woody could offer an explanation, Trish started to run off at the mouth.

"Oh, my God, did he fall over the side? Is he lost at sea? Did a shark get him? Oh, my God, I can't exactly call his parents because they're like dead, and his bitch of a sister, she like totally hates me and—"

"No, no, please calm down," said Woody. "It's not at all what you think. Mr. Sage is fine. Really. He's just resting up forward in the master stateroom."

Neglecting to catch a fish was one thing, but learning her "yachtsman" had the sea legs of a petunia was quite another. The reverberations of Trish's displeasure skimmed across Biscayne Bay and back, causing coastal disturbances in otherwise calm waters.

Woody didn't think it cool to wait around for Fred Sage to pay him. Damn fool had enough shit on his plate. Besides, at this point, he just wanted to go home, chug several beers and try to collect the scattered pieces of his recently blown mind.

Quickly gathering his knapsack and banjo, Woody disembarked the *Midas Touch* and headed for the dock house.

"Glad to see you made it back alive," said Skip as he walked through the door.

"In a manner of speaking."

"Huh?"

"Let's just say it's been one helluva long and strange afternoon."

"What happened?"

"Dude got a nasty case of seasickness. Then he popped too many pills and spent the entire trip passed out in his stateroom."

Skip burst out laughing. "Shit, I knew it might get ugly. But not like that."

"You have no idea."

"Why didn't you return to the club?"

"Sage wouldn't hear of it. This was supposed to be a fishing trip, remember? He needed proof positive for his fiancée. So guess who was elected?"

"Catch anything?"

Considering the circumstances, this was one fish tale better left untold.

"Well, I did. But, ah, Ray, ah, I mean, the fish, he got away."

The phone rang. As was customary, Skip waited about six or seven rings before picking up.

"What the hell do they want from my life now?" barked Skip, picking up the receiver. "Edwards here. Oh, hey there, darlin'! How are you doing? Is that so? I'm sure your nephew'll be thrilled. Yeah, sure thing, you take care of yourself, darlin'."

Skip handed off the phone to Woody. "It's your auntie."

"I assumed as much."

Katherine rarely, if ever, called him at work, and when she did, the news was never good.

Fortunately, no injuries were sustained.

Unfortunately, he needed to fetch his relative ASAP from the Bay Harbor Island precinct.

He could hardly wait to hear why.

With little warning, a pop-up storm converged on the Miami area. Woody tried to make a run for it, but he just wasn't fast enough. Soaked, but actually refreshed, he was about to climb inside his truck when he heard his name called. The voice was female, the accent unmistakably unique. It had to be Madalina.

Sure enough, there she was. Jogging up to him, puddles back splashing in her wake. Her foul-weather gear consisted of a small green garbage bag which provided little protection from the deluge.

"I am so glad to have catch you!" she cried. "Is possible you can please take me to bus stop, yes?"

"Of course," he heard himself say. "Hop in."

Apprehensive, but excited about the prospect of another shot after his previous one had failed, he lapsed into semicoherent babble as he climbed in next to her.

"Never expected it to pour like this after being so sunny all afternoon. There wasn't a cloud in the sky. But then again, this is Miami. Anything can happen. But it has been real humid lately. Been weeks since it last rained. Actually, more than that. Guess the winds must have shifted from the east and . . ."

He stopped midsentence. Jesus, how unoriginal was it to talk about the weather?

"Now, ah, where are those car keys of mine?"

He dug into one pocket—finding only loose change and a soggy stick of gum—and the other, empty, save for a gaping hole. Which explained why it was—well, empty. Determined not to get frazzled, he politely excused himself and stepped out of the truck. The increased intensity of the storm would make the search-and-rescue mission all the more difficult, so in order to save face and time, he fetched the extra set of car keys hidden under the back bumper. A valuable trick his uncle Herb had taught him years ago.

Woody climbed into the pickup. "Sorry about the delay."

"What is this?" asked Madalina, pointing to the injury he'd sustained the previous night.

She reached over and ran her fingers through his wet hair.

"Is hurt?"

"Not at all," he said, trying not to wince when she touched it. "Nothing. Just a bump."

"Bump?"

Boom-ped.

"You get in fight?"

"Nothing like that. Just a silly accident."

"But it hurts, yes?"

"Just a little, but I'm pretty tough."

"Me, too. I have four brothers at home, and they beat on me all the time when I was girl. See, have scar on chin from this."

"Where?"

"Right here . . ."

She put her face practically in his. So close, he had to distract himself by conjuring up the name of his third grade social studies teacher. Mr. Nader? Or was it Mr. Naddler? Adler? Stadler?

"You see it?"

"Oh, come on, it's barely noticeable."

As far as he was concerned, nothing could detract from Madalina's beauty.

"After my brother he does to me, I get even. Break his nose. BAM!"

"Whew, remind me not to get you angry."

"Not you, Voody. You are too sweet boy."

"Guess this, ah, sweet boy better get you where you need to go," he said, inserting the key in the ignition.

Needless to say, the hum of a responsive engine was naturally music to his ears.

"Your car, it is better today, right?"

"Well, not exactly."

He explained the problem with his busted air-conditioning.

"So we will roll down windows, yes?"

"But then you'll get wet."

"Does not matter. I am already very wet."

Although he knew she meant something else, this description still managed to get him harder than a fourteen-year-old on Viagra.

Woody subtly readjusted himself in the seat, pulled out of the parking lot and turned onto the service road. A quarter mile up, he reached the Trade Winds Yacht Club's main entrance where Big Bill, a former marine, was squeezed into his security booth. Woody saluted him as he did every morning and evening. Big Bill returned the gesture and then shot him an extra two thumbs-up. No doubt he'd noticed the babe in the passenger seat.

Anyway, as expected, a stagnant river of vehicles lay waiting for them outside the gates. Woody unsuccessfully searched for an opening in the rush hour traffic.

"I do not understand," said Madalina. "Do not these people see us?"

"Welcome to Miami. Voted the nation's number one city for rude drivers."

"For how long must we wait?"

"Probably an hour or two, tops."

"But bus, I will miss."

Woody's attempt at levity had fallen flat.

"Just kidding. Don't worry, I'll get you there on time."

Woody inched the truck as far forward as possible without getting hit. The next and most difficult challenge was to make eye contact with an oncoming driver who wasn't (a) talking on a cell phone, (b) picking their nose, (c) fixing their make-up, (d) having an argument with whoever it was in the passenger seat or (e) all of the above.

When this technique failed, he stomped his foot on the gas pedal. The truck lurched forward with an explosive fart and claimed a spot in the line of traffic.

Madalina screamed and nearly jumped into his lap.

"Oh, my God, did someone shoot at us!"

"No, no. Nothing like that. It's okay. Really."

Woody had this strong urge to comfort her, but kept his hands to himself. He didn't want to be accused of being too forward.

"My truck backfired."

"What this means?"

"Time to change the spark plugs."

The girl slunk back to her seat. In a way, Woody was relieved. With her so near his crotch, what if he spontaneously combusted?

"Maybe is time to buy new car, yes?"

"I'm afraid that's not in the cards."

"You have been to fortune-teller?"

"No, but I've certainly paid enough visits to my bank account to see what the future holds."

"In my country we have Gypsy lady, a Drabardi, who look for you in the coffee."

"Okay, now I'm the one who's confused."

"I explain. After your coffee is finished, Drabardi, she take your cup. Cover top with plate like this."

Madalina demonstrated with imaginary crockery.

"You put thumb on top. Shake. Turn over and put paper to, ah, ah, drain. Yes? Then you look in bottom of cup. It make many pictures, and Drabardi, she tell you what means. My grandmother, she was tzigane. Romani. Gypsy. She could make fortune for you. But she is very dead now."

"I'm sorry. Did your grandmother ever, you know, look in your coffee?"

"Yes, when I become twenty-one. She tell me I take big journey."

"And you did. You came to America, right?"

"Da, I mean, yes. My grandmother, she see also, how you call?"

Madalina wet her finger and drew what looked like several four-sided objects on the window.

"Squares?"

"Yes! Means many new homes for me. She also see man on horse who is running fast. Means true love come to me very quick and very hard . . ."

The girl turned to him and smiled rather mysteriously. Woody wasn't sure how to react. After all, the amount of knowledge he possessed about the female psyche could have easily fit inside the knapsack of a flea.

But then again, what if Madalina had given him some sort of subliminal message to let him know she might possibly—dare he think—be more than interested in him? Woody's fingers curled tightly around the steering wheel at the very prospect.

"But, wait, is more to tell," said Madalina. "My grandmother, she also see fish in cup."

Images of a particular tuna with whom he'd had an in-depth discussion earlier that day flooded his mind.

"A faaa-fish?" he asked, nearly choking on his saliva.

"You are okay? You lose color on face."

Woody snuck a peek in the rearview mirror. His previously bronzed skin had taken on the pallor of a corpse.

"I'm fine," he said, rather unconvincingly. "So, ah, what about this, ah, ah . . ."

"Fish?"

"Yes. What does it mean?"

"Money. Lots and lots of money. But there is more. This fish, he also hold two rings in mouth."

"Is that bad?"

"No, very good. Means boy and girl get together like for marriage or big business deal."

A lump suddenly formed in Woody's throat.

Specifically, a lump the size of a forty-pound skipjack tuna.

No sooner had Woody left Madalina off at the bus stop, than he had begun to chastise himself for not having the balls to ask her out. Was he that afraid of rejection?

Meanwhile, he was so distracted, he realized he was about to miss his exit. But given the kamikazelike behavior of the average Floridian driver, any attempt to cross three packed lanes on short notice might prove suicidal. Woody had no choice but to suck up his mistake and deal with 1–95 for another four agonizing miles.

Once he turned off the highway, Woody was able to exceed the speed of a three-legged tortoise. But, alas, this reprieve was short-lived when he hit another wall on Biscayne Boulevard. An accident, drug bust, construction or all of the above, he figured.

A twenty-minute crawl later brought him to the intersection of Broad Causeway, the final leg of his journey. Unfortunately, the fun was far from over when the drawbridge over the Intercoastal got stuck in the upright position!

After two hours in transit, Woody finally arrived in Bay

Harbor. He got out of the truck, stretched and winced. The muscles in his legs and back felt as if they'd been left in the dryer too long. Woody was about to head for the municipal building when he recognized Dorothy's silver Cadillac parked three cars down from his.

Ah-hah, he thought. *The plot thickens.*

Katherine and Dorothy—dressed in matching "Save the Manatee Club" T-shirts and hats—were the sole occupants of a bench located in the tiny lobby of the Bay Harbor Police Department. The two were chatting away as if they were having coffee and donuts at Katherine's kitchen table.

"Hello, ladies," he said, lumbering toward them. "What kind of trouble did you two get into this time?"

Last month it was the Anti-Big Box Rally. The month before that it was Seniors Against Off-Shore Drilling. And the month before that they got into a nasty scrap with the owner of a trendy Miami restaurant who refused to take Chilean sea bass off his menu.

"My goodness, sugar," said his aunt. "Here you are at last. I was about to rustle up a posse. Traffic must have been a nightmare. Poor dear, you look exhausted."

"Mind telling me what happened?"

"We were merely exercising our rights as concerned citizens of the community. In a nondisruptive and restrained manner. Right, Dorothy?"

"No offense, Aunt Katherine, but restrained is not a word I'd use to describe your behavior."

"Don't you be a wiseass, Clarence. Everything was just fine until someone went and called the cops."

"Please tell me you had a permit."

Katherine's failure to respond was all the information he needed.

Woody pulled at his upper lip. "So the police came and . . . ?"

"They asked us to leave," said Dorothy.

"You didn't put up a stink, did you?"

"No. We made our point and intended to leave. Especially because it'd started pouring something fierce. But then, well, we ran into a bit of a problem."

Anticipating an explanation that would veer off in many directions, Woody gave the ladies a stay of execution. Mainly because his bladder was about to burst.

He scurried off down the hallway and was about to enter the men's room when an attractive girl dressed in a navy suit and heels stopped him. She knew his name, but embarrassingly, he had no idea who she was.

"It's Kristin. You know, Dorothy's granddaughter."

"Oh, yeah, of course. Hey."

When he met her last night, she had on glasses and a bandana. Little wonder he failed to recognize her now.

"Sorry you had to schlep all this way for nothing," she said, pushing her curly blond hair behind her ears.

"Me, too. It sucked. I hate to be rude, but if you'll excuse me," said Woody, placing a hand on the restroom door. "I've got some, well, you know, urgent business to attend to."

"Not a problem."

He noticed her teeth were remarkably white and straight.

"I just dealt with the same, ah, pressing issue myself."

Bladder emptied, face rinsed, Woody returned to the interrogation room. Katherine and Dorothy were huddled on one corner of the bench. Kristin on the opposite end.

"Okay, now, where were we?" he asked.

"What the hell does it matter now anyway?" said his aunt.

"Yeah," piped in Dorothy. "What say we ditch this joint?"

"Not so fast, Grandma," said Kristin. "I do believe you guys owe Woody an explanation."

He propped up his body against a puke pink wall and crossed his arms over his chest. "If you don't mind, Kristin, I'd kind of like to get your side of the story first before hearing the, you know, the more embellished version."

"With pleasure, Your Honor."

Kristin shook a finger at Katherine and Dorothy.

"You guys are so busted!"

"Hey, we're innocent until proven guilty," said Dorothy. "What about due process?"

Kristin ignored her grandmother's comment and continued.

"I had this seminar downtown, and Grandma offered to drive me there and then pick me up later. She and your aunt allegedly had plans to shop and do lunch."

"This should have been your first clue that those two were up to no good," said Woody. "My aunt doesn't DO lunch."

"Because she's too cheap," said Dorothy.

"Oh, shut up, big mouth," said Katherine.

"Anyway, no sooner did they split," said Kristin, "than, apparently, a cop pulled them over."

"Why?" asked Woody.

"My grandmother wasn't wearing her seat belt."

"Damn thing is too uncomfortable," said Dorothy.

"That's no excuse, Grandma. Anyway, the policeman sees that her license has expired, so your aunt has to drive. Supposedly to the motor vehicle department."

"Only the damn lines were way too long," piped in Katherine.

"So they headed up to Bay Harbor," said Kristin. "For an impromptu protest against this developer's plans to build a condo and marina in a manatee-protected zone."

"Courtesy of the Hollings Group, thank you very much," interrupted Katherine. "Dirty rotten rat bastard."

"But here's what I still don't get," said Woody. "If the women agreed to leave, why did they still end up at the police department?"

"Turns out my grandmother wasn't the only one with an expired license."

Woody glared at his aunt. "How the hell could you let that lapse?"

"Don't give me lip! The truth is, I was afraid I'd flunk the eye test, so I've been putting it off."

Now it all made sense why, after so many months, Katherine left her car behind and chose, as many elder residents of Key Biscayne did, to ride her three-speed bike for any local errands and reserve big shopping trips to be shared with either her nephew or Dorothy.

"Anyway," said Kristin. "Grandma tried reaching me first, but couldn't. By the time I picked up the message, I'm afraid you were already on your way to retrieve these felons."

"Guess this would have been an opportune time to have a cell phone," said Woody.

Both he and his aunt had refused to join the masses of wireless devotees.

"Would have certainly saved you a trip," said Kristin.

"You took a cab from downtown?" asked Woody.

"Yeah," said Dorothy. "For what it cost, I could have flown her first-class back to Boston."

"Hey, don't bitch, Grandma. I wasn't the one who broke the law."

"Oh, hush you," snipped Dorothy. "All this tumult has given me quite an appetite. What say we all go grab some chow at Piccolo's?"

"Sorry," said Kristin. "But I've got a dinner date, and somebody did promise to lend me the car this evening. Or did you forget, Grandma? Like you forgot to renew your license?"

"Hit me below the belt, why don't you?" said Dorothy.

"Woody," said Kristin. "Would you mind giving these reprobates a lift back to the Key?"

Chapter 7

Todd spit his gum off the terrace of his thirty-sixth-floor apartment, lit up a joint and dialed Barry's cell to update him on the babe he'd just sent packing. In a prepaid cab, natch. Boorish in bed, the boy still had some manners.

Sure, she'd been such an easy mark, but the setup had been perfection. Dinner at Casa Tua. Drinks outside at the Shore Club. And, after a dance or two at Snatch, no wonder she let him partake of the real thing.

Hell, if he could pick real estate ops with the same expertise as he targeted his sexual prospects, the boy was bound to make his father proud someday.

Chapter 8

Woody awoke at precisely 12:38 A.M. with an erection and a sixty-pound dog lodged right under his balls. Mind you, a dog who didn't take kindly to having her beauty rest interrupted.

He lay for a while, trying to focus on the squeaky whirl of the ceiling fan in hopes of luring himself back to sleep, but the details of his dream were still too fresh to fade.

Madalina, clad in a sheer white dress, stands at the wheel of the Sea Sponge. *Woody is positioned behind her, his hands clasped over hers as they guide the boat together through a cluster of small islands floating atop a sapphire-colored sea.*

That works for me, he thought.

This tranquil setting is shattered, however, by the sudden appearance of a Cigarette boat of monster proportions. The wake is so strong, Woody is tossed into the water.

Madalina throws him a life ring, but when he climbs back into the cockpit, she is nowhere to be seen. He finds her down below, nude and sensuously draped across the dining table in the galley. Beckoning him with a peacock feather. But unfortunately, a glass wall separates him from her.

Gee, what would Freud have said about that one?

In the upper right corner, however, he notices a key card slot and frantically begins to search the pockets of his shorts. All twenty of them. Alas, each one empty.

Like this was a surprise!

He hears someone calling his name again and again. He turns around, and there, off the stern of the sailboat, sits an oyster the size of a kiddie pool, bobbing in the waves. The shell slowly opens to reveal none other than Raymond Prince seated—as well as a fish can—on a throne. Complete with ornate crown and a school of genuflecting sardines. In the Prince's mouth is an envelope which Woody is ordered to take. He hesitates at first, but accepts it. The moment he rips open the gold seal, he is instantly transported into Madalina's arms.

But as dreams are often portals to sexual frustration, Woody woke up before consummation.

Banjo in hand and trusty—albeit grumpy—beast by his side, Woody slipped out the sliding back door. With a waning moon as a guide, he didn't need a flashlight. But then again, the bay was steps from the house.

He sat down on the seawall, swinging his long, bare legs over the side. The tide was receding, and the water was quite calm. Above were clear skies and great visibility, so he could easily see the lights of Coconut Grove shining in the distance. He could feel a gentle, warm northeast breeze at his back and hear the fronds of the surrounding palm trees clicking together like castanets.

A perfect night for chilling out, only Woody could not relax until he had the answer to a very BIG question: was this Raymond Prince the real deal or a figment of his very active imagination?

The only way to find out, of course, was to engage in behavior which might, to an innocent observer, appear psychotic. But then again, Woody didn't have to worry about the neighbors spying on him. Not only had they erected thick "privacy" walls around their fortresslike McMansions, but at this hour, a large percentage of Key Biscayne residents were buried under the bedcovers with their Fedders blasting.

As for his aunt Katherine, well, even though she insisted upon cooling their house the old-fashioned way with open windows and ceiling fans, once her hearing aid was removed, that woman could sleep through the apocalypse.

Even so, Woody did a quick survey of the area. When he was convinced the coast was indeed clear, he took a deep breath and cupped his hands to his mouth.

"RAYMOND!" he shouted in a loud whisper. "MR. PRINCE!"

No response.

"RAYMOND? YOU OUT THERE?"

Still nothing.

Woody lifted his banjo into his lap. No sooner had he completed a refrain of "Foggy Mountain Breakdown," than, lo and behold, the tuna's head burst through the surface of the water. Flashing what appeared to be a toothy gill-to-gill smile.

"The Prince at your service! Roadside, no, scratch that, dockside service. Rain or shine. No request is out of line."

Sweetie, meanwhile, couldn't stop barking and snarling.

"Put a wrap on it, Rover!" demanded the fish.

In response, the dog's tail fell between her legs, and her mouth snapped shut for the duration.

"As for you, kid, shut your hole. Makes you look like a retard."

"I just can't believe you're really here."

"Hey, when the Prince says he'll be somewhere, he's true to his word."

"But then again," mumbled Woody. "Maybe I'm still sleeping and this is all just . . ."

Before he could complete his sentence, Raymond dropped like an anchor beneath the water. Seconds later the fish cannonballed ten feet up into the air, did a triple sommersault and belly flopped. Splashing both man and his beast.

"How's that for a wet dream?"

Woody wiped off his face with the bottom of his shirt. "Very funny."

"So, tell me, kid, what can the Prince do you for tonight?"

"Not quite sure, actually."

"Aw, come on, don't give me that bullshit. Of course you know. Why else would you have gone to the trouble of summoning me?"

"Well, to be honest—"

"No," interrupted the Prince. "Lie to me."

"I need some, well, you know . . ."

"No, I don't know."

Woody rolled his eyes. "Advice. I need some advice about this girl."

"That's all you want?"

"Is this a problem?"

"Of course not. I was just hoping for a bigger order. But we gotta start somewhere."

"Huh?"

"Never mind. So what about this babe? Does she rate high on the boner scale?"

"I don't exactly measure beauty that way."

"Bullshit. It's a known fact that all guys check out incoming merchandise with that third, all-knowing eye."

"You're losing me again."

"Do I have to spell it out for you, kid? I'm talking D-I-C-K! The way I see it, if the member don't mambo, then the chase just ain't worth the effort. Jesus, kid, exactly when was the last time you got laid?"

A year ago, Woody figured. Or maybe it was longer. An older woman. In town from Los Angeles to produce a commercial in South Beach or something. She picked him up at Scotty's in the Grove. Had just broken up with her husband and practically begged him to have sex with her. Said it was for medicinal purposes to "expunge" her ex from her "womb."

Meanwhile, Woody's lack of response provided the fish with all the information he needed to interpret the status of his sex life.

"Just as I suspected. You haven't had any pussy in ages."

Woody picked up his banjo and stood. "You know, maybe this was a bad idea after all."

"Wait!" cried Raymond. "You can't leave!"

There was a decided note of desperation in the fish's voice.

"And why the hell not?"

"Because in my business, you never let the customer walk away angry."

"Oh, what, so now I'm a customer?"

"In a manner of speaking, yeah, I certainly hope you are. And it's my job to keep you happy. Blissfully happy, in fact, so you'll keep coming for more."

Although the Prince failed to elaborate, Woody somehow felt compelled to hang in there a little while longer.

"So tell me, kid, what's this broad's, I mean, young lady's name?"

"Madalina."

"Unusual name."

"She's from Romania."

"New to the country?"

"Several months."

"Where'd you meet her?"

"At the Trade Winds Yacht Club. I'm the assistant dockmaster. She's a waitress at the café."

"Hmm, interesting. So what is it about her that has you, no pun intended, hooked?"

"Aside from being really pretty . . ."

"Nice body?"

"Yeah. Perfect, actually."

The fish gave a pitiful sigh. Dipped into the water for a moment and resurfaced.

"You must promise me something before we do business together, kid. What goes on between you and me stays between you and me. You must never, ever, let anybody see me in this condition. I have or *had* a reputation to uphold. Especially with the ladies. It'll kill me to become a laughingstock . . ."

"Or a science experiment."

"Not funny, wiseass. Not funny."

"Sorry."

"So will you promise me this?"

"Sure, your secret is safe. Besides, who'd believe my story anyway?"

"That's for sure. Good, I feel much better now. So go on and tell me more about this girl of your dreams."

"Well, she just has this infectious way about her . . ."

But what Woody failed to reveal—for reasons too personal

to share with anyone—was the uncanny resemblance Madalina had to someone he knew only from faded photos.

His mother.

She and Madalina shared the same green eyes, heart-shaped mouth, up-turned nose and gentle curve of the jaw. Even the color of her hair was the same. It was almost uncanny.

". . . And, shit, I can't stop thinking about her. I mean, I've never fallen for a girl like this."

"Is she crazy for you as well?"

"Not sure. I mean, she told me, several times in fact, how 'sweet' I am."

The fish smirked, or given his limited facial expressions, it appeared like he did.

"I'm afraid this is going to be a lot tougher than I assumed. Why do I get the feeling you know jack-shit about women."

Although it was a correct assessment, Woody didn't want to own up to this unfortunate fact.

"Give me a break, Raymond."

"The Prince. Call me the Prince."

"Girls just haven't been a priority 'cause I've been, well, you know, focused on other things. Besides, what would I have to offer Madalina anyway?"

"With me behind you, kid, more than you could ever imagine! I think it's time for the Prince to share with you some of his infinite wisdom."

This ought to be classic, thought Woody.

"Here's the deal. If you want to win Madalina's heart, the operative word here is S-A-L-E-S. Why, you may ask? Because most people, in particular the ladies, they hunt for a partner like they shop for a car. And I must tell you, it's all about an emotional connection."

"I see," said Woody.

"Now the car market—like the single world—is cutthroat, competitive and crowded with inventory. Shitloads of different makes, models, trim levels, performance capabilities, colors, sticker prices. So it's up to you, my green pea—"

"Hold on! First I'm a salesman, now I'm a vegetable?"

"We in the biz call someone who's new to the sales force with little or no experience—a green pea."

Woody rolled his eyes.

"So, like I was starting to say, before I was rudely interrupted, is that in order for you to move ahead of the pack, you have to create a strong buyer incentive. And in order to have that, you have to have confidence in your product. Namely yourself. 'Cause if you don't, then trying to make a sale will be like tap-dancing on raindrops. Because I'm going to tell you, kid, your defeatist attitude will get you exactly nada, noonka, nowhere when it comes to scoring."

"But it's not all about sex, you know."

The fish stared long and hard at Woody and then shook his head in disbelief.

"Uh-huh. Yeah, sure it's not."

"I mean, other things are important . . ."

"Do you want me to continue or am I just wasting my time here?"

"No, no, go ahead. I'm all ears. Seriously."

Granted this wasn't exactly your typical father/son conversation, but Raymond had surely tapped into uncharted territory. After all, Woody had been only six when his father passed away, so the subject of women never arose. And as for his uncle Herb, well, they were always too busy talking about boats, politics and history to get to the "other" stuff. And of course, there was no way he'd broach this subject with his aunt.

"Now, with the ladies," continued the fish. "Like I said before, buying a car is all about an emotional connection. This means it's up to you to provide that experience. To convince her that only you can provide what she wants in a vehicle that will not only hug the road like a newborn to a tit, but will get her exactly where she wants to go. And fast. Dig?"

"Sort of, but I'm still not sure where you're going with all this."

"Come on, you're a smart kid. It's easy. Your goal is to motivate Madalina to take you for a test drive, of course. And why do we want to do that? To give you a chance to show her what you got. To wow her. 'Cause then, hopefully, if you play your cards right, the feel of the wheel will seal the deal, and then you'll be the one in the driver's seat. Literally. Heh-heh. But before you do that, you've got to focus on your product's brand essence."

"You lost me on that one."

"What do you think comes to mind when people, specifically broads, think of you?"

"As a car?"

"No, as a person, schmuck."

Woody thought for a moment. He was never much for self-promotion.

"Well, I've got real good values. I'm a good guy. Kind, understanding. Patient. Shit like that."

"Boring," said the fish, yawning. "Give me something else."

Woody's eyes zigzagged across Biscayne Bay. "Sailing. I'm all about sailing."

The Prince thought for a moment. "Well then, you've got to get her sweet ass out on your boat."

"But the *Sea Sponge* won't be ready for at least another eight months."

"No problemo. I can fix that for you. Just ask, and the boat will be in the water, ready to go. Bada-bing."

Woody had invested far too many hours, days, months, years to pass this project off to anybody else.

"Or if you want, I can get you something bigger—a yacht. Fifty, sixty, a hundred feet. Anything you want, kid. Anything. All you gotta do is ask."

"Not an option, but I could, well, you know, borrow one at the club."

"There you go. Okay, now that we've got your buyer incentive settled, we have to determine who the competition is."

Woody certainly didn't have to do a search on Google to come up with a name.

"There is someone, I think. The son of one of the members from the yacht club where I work. Kid's a real player. Loaded. With his dad's money of course."

"From what?"

"Real estate."

The fish shook his head. "That's the name of the game in this town. Real estate is to Miami as the film industry is to L.A. Everybody's got a hand in it. Who's this kid's dad?"

"Are you familiar with The Hollings Group?"

"Of course. They've got buildings going up all over town."

Woody filled him in on the details: from the dead car battery to Todd showing up with that damn Hummer of his. And how he suspected Madalina might be out carousing with him at this very moment.

"Ah, don't worry about that snot-nosed prig. Dude may have a big trust fund, but I'll let you in on a secret. Guys who drive Hummers always have hamster schlongs."

"How could you possibly know that?"

"Hey, who do you think you're talking to here?"

"Do I have to answer that?"

"After twenty-five years in the car business, the Prince knows his shit. Which brings me to the next question. What are you driving these days?"

"An old Chevy pickup. Bought it second, well, actually third hand. Kinda beat up. Radio's shot. Air-conditioning busted. Needs new spark plugs. Alternator, iffy . . ."

"Mama mia. Why does this not surprise me? We clearly need to put you in a new set of wheels."

"Just like that?"

The Prince waved a flipper in the air. "Yeah, just like that. The Prince can make you a deal you won't forget. All you gotta do is ask."

Woody opened his mouth as if to speak and then reconsidered.

"Gee, I have to think about this . . ."

"What's wrong with you, kid? Here I am about to offer you any car you want. From a Beemer to a Rolls Royce Phantom. You want a Ferrari, you got it. A Porsche, no problem. Or maybe you could see yourself in a convertible Lamborghini Gallardo. Talk about curb appeal, that girl would cream if she saw you driving up in that. I'm thinking black exterior—elegant, yet aggressive, but discrete."

"Discrete is far from the word that comes to mind when describing a car like that. Don't you think that extravagant acquisition would arouse just a little suspicion?"

"Aw, the hell with them! It's none of anybody's business."

Woody shook his head. "There's my aunt for starters. And everybody at the club. Staff. Members. Besides, I've always worked my ass off for everything I've ever gotten, so I appreciate your generous offer, but I'm going to have to decline."

The fish's body shriveled like an accordion stuck midway through a chord.

"This is ridiculous," he whined. "Impossible. Raymond Prince never loses a sale."

Woody gnawed on a nail. "Maybe you haven't, exactly."

"Then talk to me, baby!"

"Well, the truth is . . ."

"No, lie to me."

"I really need to have my truck repaired, but I don't have the money or the time to—"

"Say no more. It's yours for the asking."

"You could really make this happen?"

"Hey, this here is the Prince you're talking to. Like I keep telling you. All you have to do is A-S-K."

Which was exactly what Woody did. Ever so politely of course.

"Kid, you've got yourself a deal!" said the fish. "Anything else I can do you for tonight?"

"What about Madalina? I'm still not sure where or when to ask her out."

"Be on the corner of South Bayshore Drive and Route One today at 6:45 A.M. and she'll be waiting for you."

And with that, the fish was gone.

As if in some hypnotic daze, Woody slowly walked to the front of the house, Sweetie faithfully glued to his side. And there, like the Prince had promised, was his Chevy looking as if it had just come off of the showroom floor!

Gone were the dings, the dents, the rust. The exterior was now shiny and meticulously buffed. The interior was immaculate as well. No more garbage strewn about. Those ripped fake-suede seats had been replaced with soft leather. That five-year-old wad of gum stuck on the floor had miraculously disappeared along with every one of Sweetie's stray hairs.

A plain white envelope addressed to him was taped to the steering wheel. Woody pulled out the note and read it:

Always at your service. 24/7.

The Prince.

P.S. Be sure to check out the glove compartment for a little cruise control.

Following orders, out tumbled a colorful assortment of several dozen condoms.

Chapter 9

Woody continued to check the clock at half-hour intervals until finally, at dawn, he leapt out of bed, showered, shaved, dressed and was on the road in ten minutes flat. Driving a fully functional vehicle involved some adjustment, but with one of his favorite bluegrass CDs blasting on the stereo and the AC cooling him off, the transition didn't take long.

Save for a few early bird commuters and a jogger, Crandon Boulevard was empty. Woody made a pit stop at the Donut Gallery (open for business at 5:30 A.M.) and ordered a "Ted's Special"—ham, bacon, cheese, tomato and egg on an English muffin. To go. Then he drove off the island to Hobie Beach—a thin strip of sand on Virginia Key popular with windsurfers and the canine set—mainly because of its proximity to the appointed rendezvous point.

In what was an atypical move for a guy who never before cared about crumbs or grease, Woody decided not to eat in his refurbished vehicle and, instead, ate under a palm tree. Alone, save for several sand fleas and a rambunctious seagull.

Seven minutes later, Woody was back in the truck. He breezed over Rickenbacker Causeway, turned onto South Bayshore Drive and stopped for a light when—at precisely 6:44 A.M.—a county bus on the opposite side of the street pulled away.

At 6:45 A.M., just as Raymond had promised, there she was, with a befuddled look on her face as if she had lost her way.

With no time to waste, Woody rolled down his window and shouted.

"Madalina!"

The girl did a double take and then waved enthusiastically.

"Voody!"

"Need a lift?"

And just like that, she dashed across the street and climbed into the passenger's seat.

"Wow! You have new truck, yes?"

"Nah, just got the old one repaired."

"So quick?"

"Yeah, funny thing about that."

Madalina stroked the dashboard as if it were Aladdin's lamp.

"Is lucky for you, yes?"

"Guess so."

"And, I think is very lucky for me to find you, Voody."

"It is?" he asked, his voice cracking.

"Yes. Otherwise I am so late for work. My stop is missed when I fall asleep in bus. I have left club far behind, I think."

"About four miles to be exact."

"Guess I don't make enough sleep last night."

Madalina didn't offer a reason for her "insomnia," and Woody certainly dared not pry.

"How about this weather?" he said, his voice again cracking. "Dry. Warm but not too hot. The wind's perfect. Not a cloud in the sky. Great day to be out on the water."

"Too bad I must work."

Woody took a much needed breath and continued. "Have you, ah, ever been sailing before?"

"No, but I have watched boats at club and I love to try."

Had Madalina actually grabbed the bait so quickly?

His left knee began to move up and down to the beat of his

racing pulse, but he still couldn't bring himself to ask the question.

Woody could almost smell Raymond Prince's brackish breath over his shoulder as the fish egged him on: WHAT THE HELL IS WRONG WITH YOU? ARE YOU A MAN OR AN AMOEBA?

"Well, maybe," said Woody. "After your shift is finished and all . . . if you don't have any plans, I'd be happy to take you out. On the bay, that is. Sailing."

Chapter 10

"And you're not to leave until you've taken care of business," said Kristin, depositing her grandmother and Katherine in front of the Department of Motor Vehicles.

"Bossy, just like her mother," said Dorothy.

"And you're not?" quipped Katherine. "It's all in the DNA, sugar."

"You and your genetic psychobabble can shove it."

Anticipating the task at hand, neither woman was in the best of moods.

Dorothy renewed her driver's license without a hitch. Not so with Katherine. The fact that she flunked the eye test came as no surprise. For the past five years she'd boycotted her optometrist. He had made the egregious "mistake" of prescribing bifocals, which Katherine was convinced she didn't need. Of course, Dorothy attributed her friend's obstinacy to another, more deep-rooted affliction.

"You cheap old coot! I told you that you should have sprung for new glasses."

"Go suck an egg. It's not about the money."

"Sooner or later, honey, it's always about the money."

Finances were a recurring subject of dissension between the

two women. Dorothy's husband, Milton, who'd hit a fatal lob on the tennis court, had left his widow pretty flush.

Katherine, on the other hand, was not so fortunate. By the time her husband passed away, his medical bills had wreaked financial havoc. Sure, she had her pension, and Woody pitched in what he could (despite her objections), but with property taxes reaching astronomical numbers, funds were always tight. Dorothy's suggestion of a reverse mortgage was unacceptable, as was selling her home, the mere thought of which gave her palpitations.

Anyway, the ladies, one in victory, the other in defeat, had just exited the Department of Motor Vehicles when Katherine squinted and stopped short in her tracks.

"Well, I'll be damned."

Dorothy looked left and right. "What are you talking about?"

"A kid I know from Grove Prep. I just have to go say hello."

She hustled off in the direction of a blond-haired lad who was jabbering away on his cell phone as if nobody else in the world was around. He was dressed in a snug-fitting pin-striped suit probably by some fancy-ass designer, Katherine figured— and an open-collared blue shirt and loafers with no socks. An outfit in sharp contrast to her orange Bermuda shorts, purple-striped top and dangly starfish earrings.

"Why, if it isn't Todd Hollings!"

Katherine—who had lost several inches in height since the last time she saw him—came up to the kid's sternum.

"Am I supposed to know you?" he asked.

"Mrs. Arnold from Grove Prep."

The boy grimaced as though he'd wolfed down mealy bug sushi with a side order of fried scorpions.

"Got to call you back, Barry," he said, slipping his cell phone into his pocket.

"Remember me, sugar?"

"How could I forget," he said.

Back in high school, Todd had been a star lacrosse player.

Only problem was all athletes were required to maintain a certain grade point average, and when he flunked Katherine's biology midterm, he was suspended from the rest of the season's games. Todd's father attempted—not so subtly—to get him a reprieve. But the way Katherine—a veteran and well-respected member of the teaching staff—saw it, Hollings was an obnoxious little shit who deserved no breaks.

"I had to go to summer school because of you," sneered Todd.

Katherine laughed. "Sorry, sugar, but from the looks of it, you survived quite nicely. In fact, I read in the alumni newsletter that you got a job working for your daddy's company."

"Yeah, so?"

Katherine felt her blood pressure rise. "Do you have any idea of the impact your father's company has on natural habitats?"

"Like I care."

"I'm sure you have no clue that delicate ecosystems are in danger of being totally degraded, fragmented and destroyed by this senseless sprawl which your daddy, among many others, is guilty of promoting."

"Whatever."

"Did you know Florida is one of three states with the highest numbers of federally listed endangered species? Wetlands are being destroyed. Birds displaced . . ."

"In case you haven't noticed," said Todd, turning to leave. "I'm no longer in your class, Mrs. Arnold."

"One more thing, young man, before you prance back to your spoiled-rotten little world. Is it true The Hollings Group is in negotiations to purchase the property on Virginia Key?"

"Now, wouldn't you like to know?"

Chapter 11

Woody had just finished rigging the mainsail and jib of one of the club's twenty-three-foot sailboats when the "Cuban Inquisition" showed up.

"Hey, man," said Ariel. "Whatsup? Going sailing?"

"Sure looks like it, huh?"

"Lesson?"

"Never on Tuesday," said Woody, craftily avoiding the trap his friend had intentionally set.

"Shit, I forgot what day it was. So you taking the *Sonar* all alone?"

"Don't worry," remarked the future solo circumnavigator. "I somehow think I can handle it."

Ariel pointed to several orange life vests lying in the cockpit and scratched his balding head. The interview was obviously not over.

"But who's that extra PDF for?"

"Leftover from the other day, I suppose."

"But something don't make sense to me here."

Oh, boy, he thought. *Here we go.*

"You never hang around this joint any longer than you gotta, and I happen to know that today you don't gotta."

"What, I'm not allowed to change up my routine once in a while?"

Woody snuck a peek at the weather-beaten Swiss Army watch he'd inherited from his father. Half past three. Madalina's shift had just ended, and she was due any minute. He had to get rid of Ariel.

"Enough about me. Why aren't you sitting on that new deck I helped you build? Smoking a cigar and working on your second Bud."

"Elizabeth's damn garbage disposal went and got busted again. Took me forever to fix the fuckin' thing."

"So go home already."

Ariel slapped his hands to his hips and refused to budge.

"Now what's wrong?"

"Tell me something, man. How many years we know each other?"

"About fifteen"

"Because I know when you're trying to blow me off. So let's cut the bullshit. I know you got yourself a date with Madalina."

Woody didn't have to ask from where Ariel had gotten this information. He knew it was from his wife, Elizabeth, who also happened to be Madalina's boss.

"Nothing is sacred around this cesspool, is it? And, just so it's clear, this is not an official 'date.' I'm just giving her, well, a free lesson, that's all."

Meanwhile, the young lady in question had just exited the clubhouse. Ariel, who must have picked up on Woody's dilated pupils and loosened jaw, glanced over his left shoulder.

"Ah-ha, guess I'll be going right about now," he said, smiling so broadly, his pudgy cheeks seemed to cast a shadow over his ears.

"You know, Ariel, please don't take this the wrong way, but I'd really appreciate it if you don't stop to chat with Madalina. I mean, I don't need you blurting out something well-intentioned, but potentially embarrassing to me. Like asking her to be extra nice to the 'poor boy' on account of his being shy or socially retarded or some such crap."

"Relax, man. Give me some fucking credit here. I won't blow your cover."

True to his word, Ariel walked up to the main dock, made a sharp right—completely avoiding Madalina—and jogged toward the office. As if he had some pressing emergency to which to attend.

In the interim, the closer Madalina approached, the louder Woody's heart beat until it sounded as if there were a herd of elephants stampeding over kettle drums inside his chest.

Woody knew he needed to get a grip. After all, this was HIS world. A world where HE felt most comfortable and in control. Where HE could shine. Show his stuff. Do his thing. And like Raymond said, this was the perfect environment for him to promote his "product" and make a "sale."

Bolstered by his pep talk to himself, Woody coolly leapt off the *Sonar* and onto the dock to greet his honored guest.

"Glad you could make it, Madalina."

"Of course I make. I tell Elizabeth how much I look forward to sailing with you."

Funnily enough, the thought of being "outted" didn't irk him as much anymore.

"Now before we get started I've got to ask you an important safety question. Do you know how to swim?"

Woody mimicked a version of the breast stroke which, had he been in the middle of the ocean, would not have gotten him very far.

"Yes," said Madalina, giggling. "I understand you now. Of course I make swim. I live on Black Sea in my country, remember? In school, I was on, how you say in English?"

"On a team? You competed in swimming races?"

"Yes, yes! I show you!"

A lock of hair fell into Madalina's face. She slowly brushed the wisp off her mouth, an act Woody found quite erotic. And then, as if this wasn't suggestive enough, she reached down the front of her T-shirt and pulled out a silver necklace from which dangled a cross, some sort of amulet and an engraved medal.

"See, I win when I make swim very fast."

"That's really cool. I'm impressed."

"Thank you." She got a concerned look on her face. "But is possible I will fall in water, Voody?"

"If we were in a much smaller boat like a pram, well, yeah, you might. That's why I chose a heavier and more stable ride like this *Sonar*. A keel boat. But even so," he said, reaching into the cockpit for a vest. "To be doubly safe, you really need to wear one of these."

Madalina held the life preserver with the tips of her fingers as if it were toxic waste.

"If it makes you feel any better, I'll put one on, too."

Madalina made a face, but followed Woody's lead. Only, her zipper jammed. This wardrobe malfunction presented a potentially sticky situation for the captain.

"You please fix for me," said Madalina, thrusting her chest out at him.

He swallowed hard at the prospect of being inches away from her, gripped the zipper and gave it several yanks to no avail.

"Is broke, yes?"

"Nah, probably just needs a little lube job."

Woody reached into his knapsack for his trusty can of WD–40. One little spritz did the trick. Being a gentleman, however, he dared not slide the zipper on Madalina's life vest any farther north than an inch.

Technical problem solved, Woody climbed onto the boat first and offered a helping hand to Madalina.

"Wait," she said, untying her Pumas. "I must remove."

"No, no, it's a lot safer for you to keep on your sneakers."

"But what about you?"

"Hell, I've been sailing barefoot ever since I can remember and—"

Before he could finish his sentence, Madalina—her shoes left behind on the dock—had deftly climbed into the boat and plopped herself down on the wooden bench inside the side deck.

"If I am to sail, I must be like you," she said.

Put this way, Woody of course interpreted her obstinacy as flattery. Although he did warn her to be careful not to stub her toes on the deck gear.

"Okay, all set then." He hoisted the main and jib halfway in preparation for casting off.

"Looks hard, what you do, Voody."

"Nah, been doing it since I was a kid. And it's not exactly rocket science. All basically boils down to knowing how to properly trap the wind in your sails. See that little red arrow up there at the top of the mast?"

Madalina nodded. "I see. What this means?"

Delighted with her inquisitiveness, he continued. As simply as possible—given the language restraints and all.

"That arrow tells you where to find the wind."

"And where it is?"

"Blowing from the land. Like it does most afternoons this time of year, providing the sun has had a chance to warm up the ground. Here, I'll teach you a little trick I use. See those ripples in the water?"

"Yes," said Madalina, peering over the side.

"If I want to guess how fast the wind is blowing, I take a good look at what's happening on top of the water. See how glossy and shiny those tiny waves are? And how they don't break and . . ."

Woody felt her staring at him. Did she think him an asshole

for going on like this? Trying to show off by explaining the Beaufort scale?

"I'm totally losing you, aren't I?"

"No, silly boy. Is good you make very much passion for sailing."

He couldn't have said it better himself.

Madalina clapped her hands. "We are moving!"

"This is nothing," said Woody, tying off the main and jib sheets. "Just wait until we get out into the open water."

"We go very fast, yes?"

"With this wind behind us, we're going to fly."

She was staring at him again. Did he have a piece of snot hanging out of his nose? Or was his zipper open?

"What means when you move stick?"

"Stick? What stick?"

It took him a second to realize to what she was referring.

"Oh, you mean the tiller."

"Yes, I see when you move tiller . . ."

Tee-a-lareh.

". . . one way, boat goes other."

"Exactly. When you move the tiller left, the bow, I mean, the front of the boat goes right."

"And when you move tiller right, boat goes left, yes?"

"Exactly. I have to tell you, most novices, I mean, people who've never sailed before, well, they find this rule hard to grasp. So, I'm, like, really impressed you figured this out on your own. In fact, maybe later, you'd be up for trying to drive the boat."

Her face lit up. "Oh, yes. I think I like very much."

Things were going way better than he ever imagined. Hell, he even made it through the channel without one tack. An event as rare as say the likelihood of ever hooking up with a girl like Madalina.

As promised, the moment they made it through Dinner Key, the whole dynamic changed. Biscayne Bay lay spread eagle and ready for them. The sun bouncing off her jeweled aqua skin.

Woody almost got a hard-on.

"Look over there," cried Madalina, pointing to a sloop, sailing so close to the wind, the foot of its jib nearly tickled the waves. "Looks like much fun! Can we do?"

"It's called heeling. Kind of freaks some people out 'cause they're afraid they'll get dumped into the water."

"I am not afraid. Besides, you tell me *Sonar* boat is heavy keel, yes?"

Not only had Madalina listened, but she had also retained the information he had fed her. The girl had looks and apparently brains as well. Unlike the majority of those airheads floating above the greater Miami area.

"You're sure you want to do this?"

"Yes, yes!"

"Okay, here's what's going to happen. When the boat starts to tilt over this way," he said, demonstrating with his body. "You've got to move, real fast, to the other side. Understand?"

"Yes, yes, I understand!"

Woody slowly brought the tiller toward him, and after he'd lured and trapped enough air into the canvas, he shouted to Madalina to jump to the windward side. An order she obeyed without hesitation. The mainsail, now weighted down with its invisible load, caused the boat to dip leeward. Madalina squealed with delight as the *Sonar* swiftly cut through the waves.

And right about then, Woody could have kissed Raymond Prince square on his fat fish lips for one helluva brilliant suggestion.

★　★　★

About a nautical mile out of the Grove, Madalina was treated to a postcard perfect view of downtown Miami's skyline.

"Is awesome beautiful, yes?"

"Uh-huh," said Woody, lying through his teeth. To him, as well as to many natives and environmentalists (his aunt included) the city of Miami was nothing but a morass of cement, steel and glass. A bunch of buildings crammed together on a carpet that was too small to accommodate anything other than a couple of palm trees, a bottle of suntan lotion and a few alligators. Towering monstrosities which unlike public roads and low-cost housing, seemed to rise overnight. This absurd imbalance of fiscal priorities really pissed him off. But, politics aside, Woody had no right to burst Madalina's bubble while playing tour guide.

"See that long bridge over there?" he asked, referring to Rickenbacker Causeway. "When I was little, I used to think it looked like a dinosaur. I'm sorry, do you know this word?"

"I know about from school. And I see on television."

"Well, to me, it always reminded me of a Brontosaurus. There's his tail on one end and then the hump of the bridge, his huge body? And there, see? His long neck."

"But head is missing."

"He's fishing. For tonight's dinner. So he's got his head under the water."

"What make you think dinosaur"—*dena sour*—"he is boy?" she asked, flashing an impish smile.

"You know," said Woody, laughing. "I don't think I can answer that question. But here's what I do know. It's time for us to change our course."

Woody's next challenge was to explain one of sailing's most basic but tricky maneuvers in a way that might not tie Madalina's brain in a knot.

"When the boat begins to turn, the most important thing is for you to watch this here," he said, patting the boom. "The moment it starts to move toward the middle of the boat, we're going to duck under and move to the other side deck."

Woody chose to leave out the part about using one's body weight to keep the boat in a vertical position after the sails begin to refill with air.

With her consent, Woody eased the mainsail halfway out and brought the boat across the wind in a beam reach.

"Ready about, Madalina?"

"Ready!" came the confident reply.

Woody uncleated the jib sheet and hard pushed the tiller away from his body.

"Helms-a-lee!" he shouted as the boom whipped over.

The moment the bow turned into the wind, he and Madalina leapt—albeit carefully—to the other side deck so the tack could be completed.

"See, now we're on a new course," said Woody, returning the tiller to the center position.

"Whew, my heart is beat very fast."

"The maneuver can be a bit intense, I'll admit. But you did great. Would you like to try driving the boat now? No rush, of course. When and if you're game."

"Of course, I can do now."

She gathered her hair into a ponytail, took a deep breath and flexed her muscles. Making it clear she was not one to wimp out.

Woody gave Madalina the helm and sat beside her, placing his hand near, but not on, hers.

"Now, the first thing you must do is pick a spot you want to sail to."

She pointed straight ahead. "There."

"That happens to be Key Biscayne. Where I live."

"So beautiful. So much green. Much difference from Miami, I think."

Thank goodness for that, he thought.

"Where is your house? Can I see?"

"Not much to look at, I'm afraid. Kind of run-down, but sits right on the water. In the meantime, try to keep your focus on your target and don't grip the tiller so tightly. Good. Make small movements. Gentle curves, almost like a dance in the water. Or like I tell my students, pretend you're drawing the letter *S*."

Woody sat back to let Madalina have a go at it on her own. Using her free hand, as if conducting a symphony, she traced her course, outlining it in the air. It was an unusual, almost comical technique but whatever worked.

"Do I go good now?"

"You're doing awesome. I had a feeling you'd be a natural at this."

"You are not making bullshit of me?"

"Absolutely not."

"I think I like very much sailing."

And just like that, for the first time since Woody decided to cruise solo around the world, he found himself fantasizing about taking on extra crew.

For those curious to learn how Key Biscayne's affluent waterfront residents lived behind their gates and hedges, the best view of course was from the water. Which explained why Madalina was having such a good time playing Peeping Tom with Woody's binoculars.

"I cannot believe houses! Just like in *Architectural*"—arc-tex-tual—"*Digest*."

She was referring to a ten-thousand-square-foot Mediterranean-styled eyesore—towering archways, Corinthian columns, Greek statuary—and its neighbor. An all-glass behemoth complete with a two-story waterfall cascading down into a swimming pool.

"And look over there," she said. "Is like, how you say, in Egypt, they have . . ."

"Pyramids?"

"Yes. How much costs this house?"

"Don't know for sure, but it's more money than either you or I could ever see in our lifetime."

"Where is your house?"

"I assure you, it's nothing at all like these others. If you look between that orange house and the purple one . . ."

To be specific, an Antebellum plantation-inspired McMansion and a two-story curved bunker with glass winglike extensions which his aunt Katherine swore was designed by a "blind ornithologist."

". . . ours is that small white ranch. Bunch of roof shingles still missing from the last hurricane. Brown lawn."

From this perspective, the residence where Woody had spent most of his life appeared squat and, as much as he hated to admit, rather pitiable. Like a disheveled urchin posing for a photo with a bunch of rich kids picked from the pages of *Town and Country*.

Madalina said nothing, but he could see the disappointment on her face.

"Now, if you look to the left of the house," said Woody. "You can actually see my boat. The *Sea Sponge*. Or at least, her beamy backside. She's going to be quite a beauty when I finish her and . . ."

"Why you have not made your house nice like others?" asked Madalina, interrupting.

Caught unaware, Woody found himself on the defensive.

"Well, first of all, the place isn't mine. It belongs to my aunt. And secondly, home improvement is like prohibitively expensive on the Key. And thirdly, to be honest, we, unlike our snotty neighbors, don't really give a shit what it looks like. All we care about is the spectacular view we've got and that it gives us the shelter we need."

"I do not mean to make dis on you, Voody. Was shit thing to do. Shame for me. My mama, she always say to me, Madalina, you speak like water run from pipe is broken."

In a contrite gesture, Madalina tenderly touched Woody's arm. Heat waves shot down to his toes and back up to his crotch, singeing the pubes on his testicles.

"You will forgive me, Voody?"

"For what? I mean, you did ask a reasonable question. I shouldn't have gotten all bent out of shape."

They sailed in silence for a few moments.

"Check this out," he said, redirecting her focus to an area about a mile off the southern most tip of Key Biscayne where a group of seven wooden structures were perched—like mutant spider crabs on legs—above the water. "It's called Stiltsville."

Woody was about to brief her on the background of this quirky part of South Floridian history when his voice was swamped by one hundred decibels of pure testosterone.

A roar so loud, the cilia lining his ear canals were flattened.

Within seconds a Cigarette boat appeared about a hundred feet off their starboard. The face of its captain—thanks to dark shades and a baseball cap—was obscured. Not so with his cargo.

One mooned white ass. Mole on left cheek. White-and-blue shark-patterned swim trunks pulled down to knees. Male.

One set of D cups. Chemically enhanced. All-over tan. Female. One belly button stud—diamond.

One set of C cups. Home-grown. Small sunflower tattoo above left hip. All-over tan.

Two identical Brazilian wax jobs.

"Whoo-hoo!" screamed D and C cups in unison, jiggling and gyrating.

The speedboat revved its 1075 twin Merc engines and then blasted off, displacing a substantial amount of salt water onto the crew of the *Sonar* in its wake.

"Son of a bitch!"

Woody was doubly pissed when he realized to whom the *Slick Whistle* belonged.

"Figures that asshole would pull a prank like that," he mumbled to himself. "Are you all right?"

Madalina seemed a bit stunned.

"Yes, I am fine. Did you know who was this person?"

"Todd Hollings from Trade Winds."

"You are sure?"

"Absolutely. That's his dad's boat."

"I see," she said, wrapping her arms tightly around her chest.

"Are you cold? I'd, ah, offer you my T-shirt, but it's not exactly dry either. Shit. Given that it's past five and we'll have the wind in our face, maybe we ought to be heading back to the club . . ."

They pulled into the Trade Winds just as the setting sun illuminated downtown Miami with such intensity the buildings seemed as if they'd melt.

Madalina said little on the long way back but Woody attributed her mood change to fatigue or perhaps lack of food.

"Hungry?" he asked after he'd secured the *Sonar* to the dock.

She touched her belly and nodded. Needless to say, the boy was psyched when she agreed to have a bite with him at Scotty's Landing, a nearby cheap joint favored by Grove locals. With Madalina's permission, he ordered conch fritters and fries. Along with a pitcher of icy cold Bud.

"You like beer?"

"I love!"

And with that, Madalina downed her mug, unsuccessfully stifled a burp and poured herself another. And one for him as well.

"In my country our beer is called *Ursus*, and people say is one of best in all of Europe."

"Interesting name. Ursus."

"Is means happiness for living every day with all your friends. Like you, Voody. You are my friend, yes?"

"Absolutely."

Of course, someday, he hoped he'd be more. But one step at a time.

"Let us drink to all my new friends here in America," she said, clicking her mug to his.

"Speaking of which, you never did tell me how you came to this country."

She lowered her chin and fiddled with the paper place mat. "I am embarrassed to say."

"Madalina, you can tell me anything. I mean, well, then again, if you don't want to . . ."

"You promise not to make judge of me?"

"I promise."

What could have been so terrible? he thought.

Had she been abducted in a sex trafficking scheme only to escape, turn informant and then be rewarded with citizenship?

Had she been a stowaway on a ship?

Had she arrived under cover from another galaxy?

Madalina took a sizable swig of beer, wiped the foam from her upper lip and proceeded to set off a bomb.

"You see, I come to America with my husband."

Woody's jaw dislodged, falling to his chest with a thud.

"Whoa, that's a surprise."

"I meet Edgar while I work as maid at hotel in my country. On Black Sea. Very luxury. Four star. He spend week there as guest and he is falling in love with me."

As it had taken Woody a far shorter time than that to fall under her spell, he fully understood that phenomenon.

"Edgar is big gentleman," she continued. "Not like all silly boys I meet who always want to make sex with me . . ."

Note to self, thought Woody. *Never push the sex part.*

". . . He treats with much respect. He call me his 'princess.' He tell my parents he want to marry with me. Bring me to America. Promise to take care of me. Even send them money to help out because I am gone."

"What did you think about that?"

She shrugged her shoulders. "We are poor family and everything is struggle. To make money. To go to store to buy food. Everybody must work two, three jobs. But is like this in Romania for many people. Is shit. Is why we drink so much, yes? No time for much fun, you understand? Is very hard for your side of world to understand what happen in my side of world."

Woody nodded. It was true. That type of life was completely foreign to him in more ways than one.

"Edgar, he promises to give life to me I never have. If I want to study at university, he will pay. If I want to go buy new dress, I can buy. Anything I want. Even so, I am still not sure. Is big decision, yes? I have never been away from my family, my home. But Edgar, he is calling, calling every day for two month until I say yes. We get married in my country, and he brings me to Atlanta, Georgia, to big house. But on first night"—Madalina's eyes welled up—"his heart is very stopped."

"Jesus. How awful. Especially for a young guy like that."

"But you see, Edgar, he is old."

"How old?"

"I am not sure exact, but seventy years perhaps."

Woody repeated the number in hopes that he had misunderstood her, but sure enough, he'd heard correctly.

"Edgar, he also has children much older than me. And," she hesitated for a moment. "I soon find out—wife."

"No way. The guy was married?"

"Yes. But wife is at place for crazy people, so he make like she is not with him anymore."

"Then what happened?"

"I am kicked out of house a week later. Abandonated. I have

nothing but green card. I sell my diamond ring at big loss to buy food, bus ticket and some clothes."

"That's awful. Why didn't you go back to Romania?"

Of course, he was secretly grateful she hadn't chosen that option.

"Is not possible. I have big shame to go home. Besides, I love America and do not want to leave. Thanks to God my cousin, Jenica, and her husband invites me to stay with them in Miami. They help me find job at Trade Winds."

"And the rest, as they say, is history."

Woody smiled at her in a way he hoped would be translated as reassuring.

"Seriously, though. I'm really glad it all worked out for you."

"Yes, but now is very hard for me to trust anyone again, you understand?"

"Under the circumstances, absolutely."

But the shitty part was that Woody knew he, too, had in a sense deceived her as well. A thick fog bank suddenly rolled in, bringing with it zero visibility and a loss of tongue. He paid the check at Scotty's and drove Madalina back to her cousin's place—a run-down apartment building in the more dicey upper reaches of Grand Street.

"Ever since I tell you about Edgar, you have been so quiet," said Madalina. "I think you do not like me now."

"Of course I do. A lot. It's just that . . ."

Woody chewed on the inside of his jaw. He knew revealing his "source" would be a far harder thing to accomplish than try-ing to right a dinghy in gale force winds, but he had to come clean. He owed Madalina as much.

"I haven't exactly been that honest with you."

"What do you mean?"

"Remember, this morning, when you asked how I was able to get my truck fixed up so fast and all? 'Cause I mean, in

Miami, where everybody moves in slow motion, it's unheard of
to get this kind of service in less than twenty-four hours."

"But why is not good?"

"Oh, it is, believe me. Awesome, in fact." Woody purposely
avoided making eye contact with Madalina. "I'm a little buzzed
right now; otherwise I'd never have the guts to tell you what
will be perhaps the weirdest story you've ever heard. And after I
finish, you're probably going to think I'm completely certifiable."

"What means certifiable?"

"Let's put it this way. Me and Edgar's wife? We could definitely hang out."

"You are crazy person?"

"I'll let you be the judge because quite frankly, I'm having
serious doubts. Anyway, this whole thing began yesterday when
I went fishing and caught—" Woody stopped and tried to gather
his wits. "Shit!"

"You catch shit?"

"No, no. A fish."

"What kind of fish?"

"A tuna. A skipjack tuna, actually. One that, that . . . well,
talks."

"Fish, he talks?"

"Yeah, as a matter of fact, he never shuts up. And guess what?
This is classic," said Woody, chortling. "His name is Raymond,
but he likes to be addressed as 'the Prince.'"

"He is like Prince Charles of England?"

"Hell no. He's just a used car salesman. Or was, until his
wife—"

"She is fish, too?"

"No, no, Italian. His wife apparently caught him with another woman and got really pissed off . . ."

"While HE was fish?"

"No, no, no, back when he was human. She, like, you know, put this major curse on him."

"And then what is happening?"

"The fish begs me to set him free. Which I did, naturally. I mean, I couldn't very well cook him for dinner, could I?"

This moment of levity fell flat. It appeared that Woody had lost his "audience."

Madalina sat back in the seat, arms crossed over her chest, deep in thought. "Why did you let Prince go without asking for him to make you wish?"

Woody was rather dumfounded by her question. It almost sounded as if she believed his fantastical story.

"Well, he did offer to give me something as a reward, but I turned him down."

She turned and leaned toward him. "Why you do this?"

"Just being a good Samaritan, I guess. But the Prince did tell me if I ever needed anything to just call and he'd be right there."

"On telephone?"

"No, on my banjo. Anyway, with my truck acting up and all, I figured what the hell, maybe the fish could help me out. I mean, I never expected him to actually make it happen."

Woody purposely left out the fact that had it not been for Madalina, he would have never entertained asking for anything from the fish.

"I know, you think I'm completely nuts, and—"

"Stop!"

Madalina slapped a hand across his mouth.

"Is possible I believe you, Voody! My parents, you see," she said, releasing her grip. "They are Romani. Gypsies. We believe in many things not of earth, you understand. I tell you of my grandmother and things she see for me in cup. You remember this?"

"Yes."

Madalina's eyes seemed to glaze over as she chewed on her pinky nail. And then she spoke.

"You must let me meet Prince."

"I, I can't let you do that."

"How can I know if he is real?"

Unfortunately, Woody had no answer for her.

She opened the car door. "I hate shit boys who lie," she said, pretending to spit.

"Let me at least explain. You see, Raymond is really vain about his looks and, well, he made me promise never to let anyone else but me see him in his, well, you know, his fish form."

"Then you must ask Prince to grant you other wish. If he really can make this magic, he will give you anything."

"But I'm a sailor. My needs are very simple. I mean, I wouldn't know what to ask him for."

Madalina planted a soft, wet kiss on his unsuspecting lips.

"You are smart boy, Voody. I am sure you can think of something, yes?"

Chapter 12

Woody found Katherine snoring in front of the TV in the living room, an impressive feat considering how high the volume was turned up. He gently roused her, but she still awoke with a start.

"Where've you been all evening, sugar?" she asked as he escorted her to bed.

"Ariel needed help on this, ah, project."

Katherine stuck her face in his and sniffed a few times. "You have beer and fried conch?"

"Yeah, stopped by Scotty's. How'd you guess?"

"Sugar, I may be a little soft in the head, but there's very little that slips by your old auntie."

After weighing the pros and cons, Woody grabbed his banjo and headed out the back door. Thanks to a low tide, the prevailing odor outside was a bit pungent. Like that of a neglected aquarium.

Woody sat down on the sea wall. No sooner did he finish one refrain of "Foggy Mountain Breakdown" than the fish du jour appeared.

"Boy, am I glad to see you again!"

"Believe me, kid, the pleasure is truly all mine. What can the Prince do you for tonight?"

"First of all, I wanted to thank you for the stellar job you did on my truck."

You had to laugh, thought Woody. *Here I am having this casual conversation with a talking fish like it's an everyday occurrence.*

"Believe me, kid, it was just the tip of the old iceberg."

"And most importantly, Madalina was exactly where you said she'd be. And at the precise time as well. It was awesome."

"Hey, who loves you? The Prince always makes good on his word. I assume you did the sailing thing like I told you?"

"Great suggestion, I must say."

"And then what happened?"

"We had a bite at Scotty's."

"Always hated that joint. Couldn't take the smell of seafood. Anyway, then what happened?"

"I drove her home."

"You score?"

"Trying to jump someone you like on a first date is so not cool."

"Why do I have the feeling there's more to this story?"

"Well, the problem is . . ."

Woody's mouth clamped shut and he stared down at the ground.

"Do you plan to tell me what happened in the next, say, year or two?" asked Raymond tapping the dark green water with one of his fins. "I'm still waiting."

"Okay, I'm just going to come out with this."

He took a beat.

"I told Madalina all about you."

Raymond's eyes grew bigger and bigger, as the color of his scaly flesh turned from blue to bright purple. Woody feared his head might explode any moment.

"Are you some kind of fucking idiot? What the hell were you thinking?"

"I just felt like I needed to come clean with her. How else could she ever trust me then?"

"You are so naïve. I guarantee that girl has a closet full of secrets. Every broad does."

Although Madalina's tale of woe had sort of creeped him out, he was so crazy for her, he had already put it behind him.

"Meanwhile I still can't believe how you could go and blow this deal after I delivered you the goods and—"

"Could you please just calm down," said Woody, interrupting. "And let me speak? Madalina didn't bail. At least, not yet. In fact, I think she might actually believe me."

"She a psycho or something?"

"No, her people are into magic and curses and shit. You know, Romanians. Gypsies. Count Dracula."

"Then the whole lot of them is psycho."

"Guess that makes me a nutcase, too, because, well, here I am talking to a, a, FISH!"

Raymond bent his head. "Point well taken."

"The bottom line is Madalina just wants proof you exist."

"Excuse me, but I thought I made it clear that save for your sorry ass, nobody, not even the Pope himself, can request an audience with the Prince?"

"Relax, she knows this isn't an option. I'm talking about something tangible. Something to convince her I'm telling the truth."

"Now here's an order I can fill. The Prince can make you a deal you won't forget. All you gotta do is ask."

"Anything?"

"Anything."

Woody shrugged his shoulders. "But I've got no clue what."

Raymond sighed. "How 'bout we trade in your pickup and

put you in a pussy magnet like a Porsche or better yet a Lamborghini?"

"We've already had this discussion. No offense, but I'm not into cars."

"Jewelry?"

"Inappropriate at this stage of the game."

"Your own private jet?"

"Don't be ridiculous."

"A baseball team? I hear the Marlins are available. Again."

"Give me a break."

"Come on, kid, there must be something you want. And please don't say 'world peace,' because this ain't no Miss Universe contest."

"Other than random stuff for my boat and my trip, I seriously can't think of anything."

"How about this? Let's say the appropriate time has passed and you want to romance the girl; where would you take her?"

"Certainly not here, to my aunt's house. Nor to Madalina's cousin's apartment."

The fish pursed his fat lips. "It seems to me you've just stumbled on the very thing you need."

Woody connected all the dots. "As in my own place?"

"Eureka!"

Woody considered this proposal for a moment. He wouldn't take her to a hotel—an option he found both sleazy and financially unfeasible. The beach was difficult, given sand fleas and possible spectators. He'd done it in his truck before, but she deserved better than that.

"Well, there's this two-story apartment building off Crandon. They have pretty cheap studios there, I think. Especially for Key Biscayne."

"Just remember, money is no object here," said the Prince.

"Don't want to be greedy or anything."

"Trust me, kid. I would LOVE nothing more than for you to be as greedy as possible."

Woody chose not to analyze the meaning of that statement.

"So you could actually pull this off?"

"I told you. The Prince can make you a deal you won't forget. All you gotta do is ask."

"Well, then, I guess I'm asking."

"And I'm giving! You'll find the passport to your love shack up close and personal."

And with that, the Prince sunk below the water.

Woody felt something in the back pocket of his shorts and pulled out an envelope. Inside he found the keys to 135 Sunrise Road and a note:

Start small. Think big.

Always at your service. 24/7.

The Prince.

Chapter 13

Woody now possessed the required evidence, only he couldn't figure out how to present it to Madalina without coming off as too brazen. One thing was for sure, the timing had to be perfect. And as anxious as he was to prove his case, he had to cool his jets. For this reason, he welcomed the multitude of tasks that kept him hustling all morning and into the early afternoon.

First there was a vintage 1968 Chris-Craft that needed to be hauled out of the water. Its owner, Mr. Ottinger—recently divorced and a major lush—had apparently run over some rocks and twisted his props useless. He had dropped anchor and waited until morning before calling for a tow. Probably so he had a chance to sober up before they towed him back to port.

Next Woody had to deal with a bawdy bunch from a reciprocal yacht club up the coast who intended to stop over in the Grove before heading southeast to the Bahamas. They had insisted upon rafting their four cabin cruisers next to each other. A major no-no at the Trade Winds, as Woody was obligated to explain. With four attorneys amongst the group, all apparently litigators, the scene got rather vocal. Needless to say, Woody was not unhappy to see them take their business elsewhere.

Then, as if this wasn't enough excitement, Chip, the five-year-old son of Roger Baker, the club's treasurer, caught—along with his dad's assistance—a four-foot-long barracuda off the main dock. Reputedly the same 'cuda that had sunk its teeth into Mrs. Stevens's left arm a year ago while she'd been scraping the barnacles off the bottom of her Hinckley sailboat. Woody's quick thinking had saved the woman's limb, but not her diamond tennis bracelet, a blunder for which she had still not forgiven him.

By 2:00 P.M., with Woody's sailing students due to arrive in a half hour and his stomach painfully empty, he headed for the café. He ordered a cheeseburger at the bar and casually scanned the restaurant for Madalina. She was nowhere to be seen.

He finished his lunch and was about to head back to the marina when he saw her. Walking in a stupor; eyes and nose visibly red. Face ashen. He jumped off his stool and intercepted her.

"What's wrong?"

"I just get call that my cousin Jenica, she has made her babies."

"You told me she was expecting twins. They're okay, I hope."

"Yes. Thanks to god." Madalina began to tear up again. "But the babies they have come six weeks early and now Jenica's mama, she will move in with them so soon I will have no place to live."

"Shit, that sucks."

Woody could feel Raymond Prince breathing down his neck. THIS IS THE TIME TO MAKE YOUR MOVE!

"Well, as a matter of fact," he said. "I just may have the perfect solution for your problem."

Woody pulled into a dimly lit parking lot located behind an architecturally unremarkable two-story cement building, circa early 1960s.

"Well, here we are," said Woody. "Nothing fancy, but a great location. The bus to the Grove is a couple of blocks away, and you can walk to the supermarket and, of course, the beach is down the road and—"

"Why do you make so soft your voice, Voody?"

"Don't want to wake up anybody."

"But is only eight-thirty."

"Well, you know, on Key Biscayne, people, they turn in early. Lots of older people live here. Retirees."

Whether or not this fact bugged her was hard to detect. She refrained from comment.

They entered the building through a narrow archway and then climbed a flight of stairs to the upper level. The entrances of eight apartments were lined up in a row—motel style. Each with matching frosted-glass jalousie-paneled doors and windows. The view from the communal balcony was not especially scenic. Below was a pool barely bigger than a bathtub, several unsteady-looking chaises and a rusted barbeque.

Apartment number 2H was distinguished from the others by its frayed doormat and the dead geranium plant housed in a chipped terra cotta pot. Woody inserted the key in the lock, but the damn thing wouldn't turn.

"Is right key?" asked Madalina.

"I sure hope so."

"Give me, I do."

True to her word, she jiggled this way and that and opened the door, and Woody followed her inside. The place must have been closed up for a while because someone had gone overboard with the lemon air freshener to mask the musty odor. Causing both of them to sneeze several times.

The layout, as per Woody's request, was certainly Spartan. A studio with an open kitchen (out-dated appliances and metal cabinets) and a tiny bathroom (blue-stained tub and sink). There was no furniture save a war-weary mattress (home to many a bedbug no doubt), orange shag wall-to-wall carpeting and a bare light bulb hanging from the ceiling. It being far from a welcoming ambiance, Woody was taken aback when she threw her arms around him.

"Is perfect."

"Really? So the Prince did good?"

"Yes, Prince, he do very good."

Madalina's good night kiss threw Woody for a loop. But the good news was that tomorrow he'd help move her into her new place, and who knew what would come next?

In the more immediate present, however, Woody had a major pair of blue balls with which to deal.

Chapter 14

Todd had no choice but to cancel his trainer. His father had "re-quested"—demanded—his presence at lunch at the Trade Winds. Some bullshit about meeting with a party planner for his mother's "surprise" fiftieth birthday bash for which she'd already found the perfect dress!

He parked in the lot and checked his watch—a rare occur-rence considering he used his Rolex as a fashion accessory and rarely as a timepiece.

"Shit! Ten minutes late," he exclaimed.

The elder Hollings would consider this act of tardiness a near federal offense, and he'd soon be calling to check on his son's whereabouts. Sure enough, no sooner had Todd stepped from the Hummer than the code name "pit bull" flashed across the tiny screen of his BlackBerry.

He didn't pick up.

Halfway to the restaurant, his mobile rang again.

He ignored the call.

Todd had no idea what the damn emergency was until he got a look at the babe sitting across from his father.

The girl, mid-twenties and a major knockout, was a planner with whom he could party. All night long, in fact. And judging from the saliva drooling from the elder Hollings's mouth, he had reached the same conclusion. No wonder his father was nervous about being seen alone with a babe like that. Gossipy club-goers would be sure to have a field day with this one unless he had someone there to run shotgun.

Todd threw back his shoulders and walked up to the table.

"Hey," he said.

"Well," said Stanford. "My perennially unpunctual son finally shows his face. Natalie, Todd. Todd, Natalie."

"Nice to meet you," said the girl, smiling.

Her white teeth—natural or bleached, he wondered—contrasted against hot pink, glossy lips. And judging from her accent, she had to be from Venezuela—Todd's number one pick for the country with the best-looking babes around. Naughty oral fantasies inundated his mind.

Natalie extended a toned, caramel-colored arm adorned with a diamond Cartier watch. Her own purchase or a gift?

There were no visual signs of a fiancé or a husband. But then again, Todd knew plenty of bombshell real estate agents who preferred not to let their male clients know they were married in order to further sweeten the deal.

"A pleasure to meet you as well, Natalie."

The aspiring suitor imprisoned the girl's hand in his.

For life.

Or at least for a few weeks of it.

Stanford Hollings, in turn, shot Todd a stare frigid enough to reverse global warming.

As did a certain waitress who happened to be on her way to their table to take their order.

Madalina was not happy when Woody met her after work. From what he could understand amidst the torrent of English and Romanian profanity, she had had the misfortune of waiting on Todd Hollings, his "slut date" and some other "asshole man."

Not only had they mistreated her, but when she accidentally (on purpose?) spilled iced coffee over the girl's white capris, an altercation had ensued.

"Elizabeth didn't fire you, did she?"

"No, she make nice for me, but I am still so pissed on shit people that make me feel I am nothing! Nothing!"

And with that, Madalina fell into Woody's arms. Hysterical. He lifted his hand, withdrew it, reconsidered and then boldly stroked her back.

"I hate to see you so upset like this. Can I do anything to, well, you know, make you feel better?"

Madalina indelicately swiped her nose. "You will do anything, Voody?"

"Whatever is in my power. Yeah, sure."

"Then you must go back to Prince."

"But, but why?" he asked.

This was one request for which he was not prepared.

"You must ask Prince for penthouse in South Beach at Summit. Is new hot building I read about in *Ocean Drive* magazine. You know this one? Is looking like stone castle in sky?"

"But what about the apartment on Key Biscayne?"

"Give back."

"I'm not sure if I can do that, Madalina."

"Then maybe I do not believe you about your fish. And maybe apartment you show me is trick. Is belonging to someone else. You just get it so you can make sex with me and—"

"That's not true. I mean, not that I don't want to, you know, be with you. That would be awesome but . . ."

This is not coming out right, he thought.

"The fish, Raymond, I mean, the Prince, I'm telling you, Madalina, he's the real deal. He offered me anything I want and . . ."

Woody slumped back against the hood of his truck and stared down at his paint-splattered Top-Siders. Madalina, in turn, cozied up next to him and seductively positioned her tear-stained face near his. He could smell her strawberry-flavored lip balm and ached to kiss her. Fat chance of that happening now.

"But you tell me you have saved Prince's life."

"Yes, I did."

"Then he will be happy to give you other wish, yes? Is no big sweat."

When Woody failed to answer, Madalina abruptly turned and began to walk away. "I don't like boys that lie," she said over her shoulder.

Chapter 15

"Just when the Prince here was about to romance a blowfish, you had to go and interrupt?"

"I'm speechless."

"Relax, kid," he said, laughing. "The Prince was only messing with you. You know I'm always happy to see you."

This confession caused Woody relief and then distress. How would Raymond feel this way after he placed another, much bigger, order?

"So tell me, how'd it go with the babe? You score?"

"Ah, not exactly."

"Shit, I knew she'd think that place was a dump."

"Madalina seemed to like the apartment at first, but then the next day, well, things changed."

The fish listened with great interest as Woody filled him in on what had transpired.

"So what you're saying is that you want to trade in."

"More like a major trade up, I'm afraid."

"No sweat. The Prince can make you a deal you won't forget. All you gotta do is ask."

Woody inhaled deeply.

Focused.

Aimed.

And fired.

"I'd like a penthouse apartment at The Summit in South Beach," he said with machine-gun rapidity.

Anticipating reprisal, Woody took cover, but nary a scale on the fish's body shifted.

"The Summit, huh? New on the market. Quite a joint. The pinnacle of luxury as they say. Our girl has clearly done her homework. Furnished or unfurnished?"

"Definitely the former for sure," said Woody, remembering the less-than-inviting interiors of the apartment on Sunrise Road.

"Whaddya say I have Madalina there at the condo, waiting for you? Beam her up *Star Trek* style. Then she'd really believe you're on the level."

"That'd be awesome."

"And how 'bout a snazzier car to go with your new digs?"

"Nah, my pickup is cool. Besides, you've done so much already."

"Hey, kid, I'd like to think we're just getting started here."

"I must tell you. I'm very appreciative of all this."

"Believe me, the feeling is mutual. I need you just as much as you need me. Anyway, just remember, kid, I can deliver the buyer to the showroom, but it's up to you to close the deal."

"I understand."

"So?" asked the fish, staring at him, rather impatiently.

"What?"

"The Prince can make you a deal you won't forget. All you gotta do is ask. Blah-blah-blah. You know the drill."

Woody reiterated his intentions. And with that, the Prince spun around and around like a whirling dervish into the purplish black waters of Biscayne Bay and vanished.

Sweetie woofed several times and nudged her head into her master's thigh. Her intention, as Woody was soon to discover, was to direct his attention to a packet hanging from a red ribbon around her neck.

Inside, he found the following items:

1. A gift certificate for two at the Blue Door in the Delano Hotel compliments of one Raymond Prince.
2. A toothbrush.
3. A set of keys clipped to a tiny jeweled crown.

As well as a note which read:

If you build it, she will cum.
Always at your service. 24/7.
The Prince.

Chapter 16

Woody floored it the moment he hit Rickenbacker Causeway. This burst of speed, however, attracted the attention of a representative of the Miami–Dade Police Department who slapped him with a two-hundred-and-fifty-dollar fine. Woody's first ticket since the twelfth grade. This blip on the radar screen succeeded in physically cooling his jets but did nothing to keep his heart from racing ahead of him.

When Woody finally made it to Washington Avenue, a hair before midnight, the area was already mobbed with that demographic upon which South Florida's economy depended—tourists. Mulling around the many clubs and lounges, anxious to get their parties started. As for the locals—specifically the "in" crowd—well, most were just sitting down to dinner.

A cluster of contemporary skyscrapers sit at the very tip of South Beach and offer many a demanding buyer the best of everything in condo living. For a hefty price. Woody's eyes scaled The Summit's glass walls. Aside from the Cape Florida lighthouse on the Key, he'd never been higher than the tenth floor of Dorothy Little's apartment! But with Madalina hopefully awaiting his arrival, this was no time for a bout of acrophobia!

Woody removed his foot from the brake and followed the red-bricked road up to a glass gazebo surrounded by multi-colored tropical vegetation. He stopped the truck in front of the security guard—a tanned Frankenstein minus the hardware. *The moment of truth has arrived,* thought Woody, expecting to be turned away. Instead the guard flashed a beauty queen smile and waved him through the gates.

Woody was welcomed at the main entrance of The Summit by a six-foot-five Aryan youth in Lederhosen.

"Good evening, Mr. Woods," said the valet, opening his door.

Shit, he knows my name.

"May I park your truck?"

Woody stared at the valet, briefly, chuckling over the absurdity of the moment.

"Yeah, sure, I guess. Ah, thanks," he said, handing over the keys.

"You're sure about this, sir?"

"At this point, I must tell you I'm not exactly sure about anything."

Meanwhile, the lobby of The Summit was as majestic as the name implied, with a ceiling at least four or five stories high. The furnishings, however, were strictly minimalist—several black leather and chrome couches placed within miles of each other and a highly lacquered console behind which stood two men in crisp white shirts and quilted red vests.

"Good evening, Mr. Woods," said the plumper of the two.

A name tag in the shape of a mountain peak identified him as *Juan, Concierge.*

"Hey," said Woody.

"May we help you with something, sir?"

"It's okay. I'm cool."

This, of course, was far from the case. In fact, he felt as if he were about to climb Mount Everest. Bare-assed without a compass. During a blizzard.

"Well, have a good night."

"You, too, sir," said Juan.

And with that Woody headed for the elevators.

In the wrong direction, as he quickly discovered.

Forced to backtrack, he nonchalantly waved to the concierges. They looked at him as if he were stoned.

Not that any South Floridians would find anything wrong with that.

An elegantly attired gray-haired gentleman and a bejeweled, miniskirted blonde half his age joined Woody at the elevator banks.

Not that any South Floridians would find anything wrong with that.

Feeling a bit self-conscious in his tattered polo and paint-stained shorts, Woody mumbled a good evening to the couple. No response was offered. Perhaps they didn't speak English, he thought.

Not that any South Floridians would find anything wrong with that.

Save for the sound of the girl fumbling through her cavernous gold handbag, it was a silent journey upward.

Funnily enough, these two were also headed for the thirty-eighth floor. Woody invited the couple to exit first. They headed left, so naturally, he opted to go the other way. The right decision, fortunately.

Penthouse H was located at the end of the oriental-carpeted hallway. Woody fished in his pocket for the keys, changed his mind and rang the buzzer.

And just as the Prince had promised, the door opened and there she was. Wearing nothing but an oversized Madonna T-shirt.

He nearly got a hard-on.

"VOODY!" cried Madalina, throwing her arms around him and planting her lips on his.

"I was in bed tonight, my eyes close, and next I know, whoosh, I am here. My suitcases, too. Everything. Is fantastic! Prince Fish, he is true. You are lucky, lucky boy."

"Guess I am, huh?"

Perhaps her definition of good fortune differed from his, but at this point, who cared?

"Come, I give you tour of apartment. You cannot believe how beautiful."

Still reeling from her kiss, he would have blindly followed her into a fetid outhouse in the Sahara and found it aesthetically pleasing!

"Condo is over two thousands square feets. And see windows? All floor-to-ceiling."

Madalina made note of some of the furnishings: a serpentine sofa covered in zebra skin, lion-clawed purple velvet chairs, a massive marble table suspended in the air by a beefy, gilded gorilla and floor lamps fashioned from elephant tusks. Your basic Tarzan-does-Vegas decor. Woody chewed on a nail to keep from cracking up.

". . . And here is custom European designed kitchen." She opened one of the cabinets. "See, comes with dishes and pots and pans. Everything. First class." She sensuously ran her hand across the counter. "Granite. Very expensive. Top-of-line stainless steels appliances. Built-in Miele espresso machine . . ."

Madalina sounded as if she were reading the copy off of a promotional brochure for the place. Like Raymond had said, the girl had certainly done her homework.

Next on the tour was the master bedroom—equally as garish as the living room. There was a king-sized circular bed draped with a white mink throw and tons of pillows, and a faux fireplace in which a faux fire burned.

"Is awesome, yes?"

"That it is," he said. "Totally."

"And you have not yet seen unparalleled Miami skyline from wraparound terrace! Come, I will show you!"

Given his squeamishness about heights, Woody would have liked to decline the invitation, but he didn't want to come off like some kind of wuss.

Outside, there was a balmy breeze blowing from the Atlantic which, given the hour, was now bathed in total darkness. To the far left lay a cornucopia of neon lights from South Beach stretching all the way to Hollywood. Although certainly impressive, the view seemed surreal to Woody. A reflection of his current state of mind, he figured.

"And tomorrow morning, we can have breakfast on terrace with all Miami at our feet," Madalina said without quivering one eyelash.

Was he hallucinating, or was this actually an invitation to spend the night with her? *Steady as she goes,* he cautioned himself. *Don't make any assumptions yet.*

Madalina suddenly rose to the tips of her bare toes and spread her arms wide as if ready to swan dive off the balcony.

"I feel like queen of world!" she shouted. "And you, Voody, are my king, yes?"

"Really?" came the unconvinced response.

Madalina turned to him and sinuously glided her breasts back and forth, down his body to that area in between his thighs, which, giggling, she brushed up against. Hard.

"I think you may be, how they say, up for challenge?"

Woody lifted his head from the pillow and squinted into post-dawn sunlight. He certainly hadn't expected to crash in the second bedroom. But unfortunately, what had begun as an erotic fantasy on the terrace never progressed beyond a PG rating.

Woody, for one, would never push the issue. Win her heart first, and then, he figured, the rest would fall into place.

He reached inside his boxers and tried rather unsuccessfully to rearrange himself. Seeking relief, he bolted from the bed to the shower. He reemerged ten minutes later, refreshed, his sexual frustrations alleviated at least for the moment.

Woody found Madalina on the terrace. Wrapped in purple terry cloth, she seemed mesmerized by the landscape below. He stood for a moment and stared at her profile. Admiring the curves of her face in contrast with the sharp definition between her jawline and her neck.

"Morning, Madalina," he said, loud enough for her to hear but soft enough not to startle her.

She turned to him, smiled and then pouted.

"What, no kiss? You do not love me anymore?"

"Of course I love you."

The words slipped so easily out of Woody's mouth, he had no time to catch them. He had never made such a declaration to anyone other than his adoptive parents and the three dogs he'd parented throughout his life. But now that his secret was out, what would be his next move?

"Breakfast," he exclaimed, his defense mechanisms clicking into place. "Want to go get some breakfast? I'm starving."

Chapter 17

Katherine figured something was up when she discovered Sweetie lying on the pillow next to hers.

"Where's Woody?"

The dog looked at her as if to say, *Beats the shit outta me.*

Katherine slipped on her robe and shuffled over to her nephew's room. The door was ajar. She knocked several times and called his name. No answer. Ignoring the NO TRESPASSERS sign which had hung there since middle school, she entered what she referred to as the "pit." Woody may have kept his boat neat and tidy, but his room could have easily been declared a disaster area.

His bed was made, however. Katherine had changed his sheets the day before and those hospital corners were still perfectly tucked into the twin mattress.

She checked to see if his truck was in the driveway. It was gone.

He'd been known to occasionally camp out on the *Sea Sponge* but not without his dog. Those two were inseparable.

The evidence was conclusive.

Woody had definitely spent the night someplace else.

But then again, although he tended to keep his private life, private, Woody still hadn't given her any indication that he might be interested in some young lady.

Not that there was anything wrong with that.

He was a grown boy.

No, he was a grown man, damn it!

Judging from the horror stories Katherine and her late husband had heard from other parents, they considered themselves very lucky. Sure, there were times when he had gotten himself into mischief, but all in all, he was a very good kid. Responsible and well-mannered.

Woody could have easily gone to the dark side. Being an orphan, he had the usual textbook issues—fear of abandonment and an inability to trust. Many kids would have rebelled, their actions fueled by anger. Not so with Woody. If anything, he had always had a tendency to cling a bit tightly to his guardians. Little wonder Herb had encouraged his nephew's plan to circumnavigate the globe. The ultimate act of independence.

Meanwhile, as long as that boy was still under her roof, Katherine couldn't help but worry. In fact, she had just pulled out the phone book and was just about to begin checking local hospitals when the phone rang. It was Woody.

She hadn't meant to, but she let him have it.

He was, he assured her, perfectly fine. With all his limbs and digits intact.

End of conversation.

Or was it?

"You still pissed at me?" he asked, kissing his aunt's flour-sprinkled cheek.

Katherine merely harrumphed and continued to chop carrots on a slab of butcher block older than he.

"Uh-oh, that answers that question."

He lifted the lid of a cast iron pot on the stove and peered inside. The smell of caramelized onions was intoxicating.

"What are you making?"

"Short ribs."

"Shit."

"Since when do you use that adjective to describe your auntie's cooking?"

"Since never. It's just that, well, I've got plans."

"I'm sorry, I just assumed. But fear not. Dorothy will be more than happy to fill in for you at the dinner table."

Katherine scooped up the carrots and stirred them into the meat.

"You got a hot date tonight?" she asked, wiping her hands on that silly apron of hers. The one with dancing lobsters.

"Maybe," he said, dismissively. He still wasn't about to tell his aunt about Madalina.

"This is news worthy of the front page of the *Herald* and all I get is a 'maybe'?"

"Need to go shower up, but," he said over his shoulder as he scurried from the kitchen. "But I'd be real appreciative if you could walk Sweetie in the morning again for me."

Dorothy scooped more mashed sweet potatoes and collard greens onto her plate.

"Jesus, this stuff is sure to give me gas, but who cares? Got no hot man in bed with me tonight. Anyway, back to Woody. It took my son Mark almost two years before he finally introduced me to Bert."

"Why, because Mark was afraid you'd bite his wife's head off?"

"I was right about that bitch, wasn't I? He's lucky to be rid of her. Even though it cost him a damn fortune. Anyway, don't nudge the boy. When he's ready, he'll tell you about his lady friend."

"But something still isn't sitting right with me. I just have this feeling he's hiding something."

"Maybe this 'she' is a 'he.' My nephew Alex had us all fooled when he came out of the closet. Had this whole secret life and—"

"Up yours, Dorothy," said Katherine, interrupting. "My boy isn't gay. But he sure is up to something."

Chapter 18

The Blue Door, with its soaring high ceilings, billowy curtains, snow white leather banquettes, pearl candelabra and Swarovski crystal in-laid votives, was one of the best rooms in town.

Todd smiled at the lanky Ethiopian beauty stationed outside the restaurant. With three martinis under his belt, he was feeling pretty damn good.

"You're new here, aren't you?"

He tried to make it his business to be on a personal level with the key staff at the most trendy restaurants and clubs.

"Yes, sir," she replied, combing her cropped, dyed-blond hair with her fingers.

"Were you in *Ocean Drive* last month modeling swimsuits?"

Step One: flattery and charm.

"Thanks for the compliment, but I'm not a model. I'm actually working my way through law school."

"Now, that's a waste of a beautiful face and body," said Todd.

Judging from the girl's reaction, he figured she was probably a dyke.

Step Two: demand.

"Here's the deal, sweetheart, I need a table for four tonight."

As in him, Barry, and the trust fund twins, Babs and Brooke Flagler, whom they hadn't seen since prep school. With their new nose jobs, lipo and boob enhancements, Todd actually entertained the idea of fucking either one of them.

"Do you have a reservation, sir?"

Step Three: push.

"No, but I'm sure you can find us something, right?"

"Actually, no, we're booked solid."

Step Four: bribe.

Todd slipped the girl a couple of twenty-dollar bills. "How about that cancellation you just got?"

She pushed the bills back to Todd. "I'm sorry, but I can't take this."

He looked at her in disbelief. "What the hell is your problem?"

"Dude, chill," said Barry, whispering. "It's okay. We can go someplace else like—"

"No," said Todd, interrupting. "I want to eat here! Jesus, you'd think after all the bucks my family has dropped in this restaurant that somebody could find me a fucking table!" He turned back to the girl. "I need you to find me Constantine."

Step Five: threaten.

"You mean the manager?"

"No, sweetheart," snapped Todd. "The fucking Pope!"

"It's not necessary to get nasty, sir, and I'd appreciate it if you lowered your voice."

"I asked for Constantine; now where the hell is he?"

"Mr. Margolis is out this evening with the flu."

Meanwhile, the Flagler twins—Brooke in her size two black mini and Babs in skinny jeans and a halter top—had finally reemerged from the ladies' room after fifteen minutes. Snorting coke, no doubt.

"We need food!" demanded Brooke.

"Yeah. Is our table ready?" asked Babs. "Huh, Todd the wad?"

Young Hollings earned this nickname back in high school, and it had stuck—no pun intended—all through college.

"I'm workin' on it," he snapped.

Todd was about to suggest that Barry take the girls over to the bar across the hall for a cocktail when he noticed a couple exiting the restaurant. What the hell were they doing there?

"Madalina," he called, leaping across their path. "How nice to see you. And, Woody, dude. Damn, I had no idea we paid the Trade Winds' staff enough money to be able to afford dinner here."

After an hour of serious dry humping on the sofa, Woody's crotch was rubbed pretty raw.

"Would you excuse me for a moment," he said, limping off to the bathroom.

He dropped his pants, positioned himself over the sink and turned on the faucet. The second the icy water hit his red and swollen dick, he had to clamp a hand over his mouth to keep from crying out loud. This technique, although harsh, managed to bring him some relief.

Madalina was still draped across that zebra-skinned couch when he returned to the living room.

"You are okay, Voody?"

"Yeah, but it's after midnight and—"

She jumped up and clung to him. "Let's not go to club to-morrow. Let's stay at apartment. Sleep late. Go to beach."

"Believe me, I'd love to, but Sundays are nuts at the club. It just wouldn't be cool to blow everybody off. We both have this Monday off, so we can definitely hang out then."

She didn't have to say anything. Her body language spoke volumes. The girl was not happy with him.

"Well, then, I guess it's good night." Woody gave her a peck

on the lips (anything more lingering and he'd never leave) and
was about to walk toward the front door when she grabbed his
arm.

"Where are you going?"

"Home to sleep, of course."

"Is way too late for you to drive home, Voody. You must
stay here. Besides, I will miss you if you leave."

Put this way, Woody couldn't possibly turn down Madalina.
Despite his being banished to the second bedroom once again.

Woody had just fallen asleep when he was awakened by
Madalina. Standing next to his bed wearing nothing but black
panties and a "wife beater" undershirt.

"What's wrong?"

"I have terrible shit dream," she said, sniffling. "Is awful."

"Do you want to tell me about it?"

She lay down on top of the covers and snuggled up close to
him.

"I dream we make big, big fancy party. Is fantastic. Many famous VIP are there. And movie stars, too. We are dressed up, and
everybody is saying what beautiful couple we are making as we
dance . . ."

"Is that where the nightmare started?" he asked, chuckling.
"I mean, I'm pretty scary on the dance floor."

Madalina ignored his comment and continued.

"But then Todd is at party. He is with all his stupid silly
friends. They make big joke from us. They say, 'Who do you
think you are? You are nothing but shit.' Everybody in party
starts to laugh and point fingers at us. Is awful. They say to me,
'Go back to your country. You do not belong here.'" She began
to sob. "Is this true, Voody?"

He wrapped his arm around her and pulled her close. "No,
of course not."

"You will not leave me, will you, Voody?"

"Not in this lifetime."

"Because you love me, yes?"

"You know how I feel about you."

"And you want to do everything to make me happy, yes?"

"Everything in my power," he heard himself say.

"Then you must go back again to fish."

Chapter 19

Woody made a habit of pickling the *Sea Sponge*'s deck with salt water every other day to keep her sun-baked timbers from drying out. But after nearly a week of neglect, it took ten buckets (twice the normal amount) and ten trips up and down the ladder to moisturize the wood. Woody considered this penance for allowing another "woman" to steal his heart.

He went down below and inserted a Chopin CD into the boom box. Sitting on the floor amongst some of his most intimate "friends"—his wooden planes, chisels and curved-claw hammers, his handmade mallets—he rested his back against what would eventually become a dining banquette. Sweetie cuddled up close and laid her head on his lap.

"Not sure if I would do that if I were you," he said to her.

That night Madalina had insisted upon making him a traditional Romanian dinner. Some cornmeal thing called "mamaliga," and "sarmale," which was cabbage stuffed with beef, rice, onions and peppers. Nobody other than his aunt had ever cooked for him before, and he was really impressed. Only problem was, although tasty, the food gave him a bad case of gas.

The dog—who was often prone to the same problem—cut her master some slack and stayed put.

Zoning out, Woody yawned and shut his eyes for what was supposed to be a few minutes.

He reopened them.

Two hours later.

In a panic.

Woody gazed at Biscayne Bay. The water was particularly black and thick tonight. Like a cauldron filled with boiling crude oil. He wasn't sure which smelled worse. His farts or the stench of rotten eggs in the air.

A harbinger of bad things to come? Or was he just being paranoid? He concluded the latter, picked up his banjo and did his thing. Moments later the fish's head burst out of a rolling wave.

"So did we turn that girl into a believer or what?"

"I'd say so," said Woody.

"Bet she worships at your altar now, doesn't she?"

"Excuse me?"

"Do I always have to spell everything out for you, kid? Did you score?"

"We made out a lot. She's an amazing kisser."

"And you're telling me nothing happened?"

"Well . . ."

"Did you have trouble raising the bridge or something? I mean, aren't you a little young to have problems in that department, kid?"

"Whoa, hold on. There's nothing wrong with my, you know."

"She at least blow you?"

Woody played with a thread hanging from the hem of his shorts and ignored the question.

"Nada, huh? So let me get this right. After giving her this

castle in the sky, the only thing you got in return was a major case of blue balls."

"She just wants to take it slow. I mean, maybe it's a religious thing or . . ."

"Bullshit," said the fish, interrupting. "I can't tell you how many parochial school girls used to genuflect between my thighs. Not to mention those church-going minxes who were supposedly 'saving themselves' until they got hitched. They used to ride me like a rented mule."

"But Madalina is different."

"Wake up and smell the pheromones, kid! I guarantee she ain't no virgin."

Woody had no intention of sharing any details of Madalina's short-lived "marriage." For more than one reason.

"Look here, Raymond—"

"Prince. Call me Prince."

"Despite what you may think, if I really wanted to go out and get laid, I could. But with Madalina, well, I respect her as a person and—"

"Uh-uh. I think the boy is in love."

Woody put down his head. "I've never felt like this about any girl. Ever."

Raymond grasped his heart and steadied himself from falling head over tail. "Whoa, this here is serious shit."

"I'd appreciate it if you didn't make fun of me."

"Whew, so sensitive. Okay, okay. I'll keep my mouth shut."

"Don't make promises you can't keep. Speaking of which," said Woody, clearing his throat. "Last night, I took Madalina to that Blue Door restaurant."

"I thought the gift certificate was a nice touch. Did you get the mango pork? Oh, man. Is that good." Raymond smacked his mouth. "Or the beef with gorgonzola sauce? And for dessert, did you try the chocolate cake or the dulce de leche spring rolls with vanilla and cachaca sauce? I miss their food so much, I think, given the choice, right now I'd actually choose a meal there over getting laid."

"Are you finished?" asked Woody.

Raymond sighed. "Yeah."

"Madalina had the lobster, by the way. And I had the grouper."

Disgusted, the fish spit into the water.

"Anyway, the thing is, we had a run-in with Todd Hollings and some of his equally reprehensible friends. Copped some major attitudes. Made fun of our clothes. Madalina went a little ballistic."

"Can't say as I blame her. I would have ripped them all new assholes!"

"I did everything in my power not to. Anyway, she had this horrible nightmare and—"

"Kid," said the Prince, interrupting. "I know this whole monologue is all going somewhere, somehow, someday. But do you think you could get to it before spawning season begins?"

"Okay, okay. You know Star Island, right?"

"Yeah, of course. What do you take me for? Some hillbilly from West Virginia?"

"Certainly not in your present state, nobody would."

"Not funny, kid. Not funny."

"Madalina read this article about this couple who live there, the Flipensterns. Pippinsteins. I don't know. Something like that . . ."

"The name you're mangling happens to be Flipengers. One of my kids went to school with their daughter. You wouldn't have believed the sweet sixteen they threw for that little spoiled twerp. Kid's dress alone cost ten grand! Took over that club Mansion. Would you believe they even got Britney Spears to sing! I've been in their house, and it looks like a fucking palace."

Woody grunted and groaned. This was going to be a lot harder than he expected.

"What's your problem, kid?"

"It's just that, that . . . well, Madalina now has got it into her head that we should have a house like that on Star Island, too."

The fish's eyes narrowed. He uttered not a word. Woody felt a rivulet of perspiration travel down his spine.

"I knew this was a bad idea. Why couldn't Madalina just be content with that damn penthouse and leave it at that?"

"Because broads, they lack the genetic makeup to be satisfied. Why do you think they complain all the time? Now, as far as this proposal goes . . ."

Woody prepped himself for rejection.

". . . I'm just loving it!"

"You are? You do?"

"Why are you so surprised?"

"I mean, come on, this is such an absurdly excessive request."

"Not at all. In this town, where you live defines who you are. And with a trophy property on Star Island, hell, it's the ultimate fuck-you to all those schmucks who think their shit don't stink. Madalina is one smart girl, and I must say I really dig her style."

"Hey, don't get any ideas," said Woody, laughing. "She's mine."

"Correction—will be yours if you give her what she wants. Just remember, the Prince can make you a deal you won't forget. All you gotta do is ask."

"Okay, then, let's go for it. Let's give Madalina that palace."

"With all the bells and whistles?"

"Yeah, sure, whatever it takes."

"Well, get your ass moving, kid! Madalina is waiting for you at Number Six Star Island Drive."

Needless to say, Woody ran, not walked to his truck. But the

Chevy was nowhere to be found. In its place was a black Porsche 911 convertible—six-cylinder, all-wheel drive, capable of doing sixty miles per hour in less than four seconds. A veritable wet dream on wheels for many an automotive enthusiast.

Not so with Woody, who had always favored secondhand pickup trucks. The thought of spending anything but bare minimum on a vehicle just didn't make sense. Boats, of course, were a completely different story.

Anyway, with no other transportation available, the Porsche would have to suffice.

He noticed a small package sitting on the driver's seat. Apparently from Hermés, a store with which Woody was far from acquainted. Along with a note:

> *You must look the part to play with the big boys. Always at your service. 24/7.*
> *The Prince.*

He opened the box and found a wallet made from cowhide as soft as the downy hair on his dog's belly. Stuck inside one of the slats was a black American Express credit card fashioned from anodized titanium. The name Clarence Woods was engraved on the front.

The good news? Woody had just earned membership in a very elite group of American consumers.

The bad? Life was about to get a lot more complicated.

Chapter 20

The sensation of driving in a Porsche with the top down gave Woody a thrill he was almost embarrassed to acknowledge.

Being a sailor, he was accustomed to dealing with air currents; but here, in this convertible, peeling down the road at 65 mph, the sensation was like none he had ever experienced:

The whooshing sound inside and around his ears.

The force with which the wind tugged at his hair and pulled back the skin on his cheeks, causing his eyes to tear up one moment and dry up in another.

The way the wheels of the sports car hugged the tarmac and executed each turn with pinpoint precision.

The inimitable song of an engine and exhaust system only a one-hundred-and-twenty-two-thousand-dollar vehicle could provide.

He looked over at Sweetie and laughed. With her fur flying and her lip curled upward in the throes of ecstasy, the dog was apparently enjoying the experience as much as he.

Meanwhile, Woody was amazed at all the attention the Porsche received:

An older woman in a white BMW nearly ran him off the road in an attempt to catch his eye.

Six barely legal girls packed in an SUV flashed their boobs in hopes that he'd "party" with them.

Some teenage boys in a red Corvette tried to challenge him to a drag race (an offer he declined).

But when a couple of drag queens in a pink Cadillac convertible pulled alongside him and screamed, "Hey, cutie, wanna blow job," Woody was more than relieved to make a left turn off MacArthur Causeway.

Star Island, a man-made oasis (circa 1922) for the obscenely affluent, was connected to the mainland by a bridge so narrow it appeared more suitable for pedestrian traffic than vehicular. Curiosity seekers were strictly forbidden, and security was extremely tight. Woody, however, was welcomed onto the island as though he'd lived there all his life. It appeared the Prince had once again pulled off another miracle.

There were only thirty properties on Star Island. Each one was set back from a single loop of road lined with forty-foot royal palms. It was virtually impossible to get lost in this tiny community. Even so, Woody managed to drive past Six Star Island Drive on the first and second takes before he figured out the residence was not identified by a postal address but by a moniker. The name—La Connerie—was affixed to a twenty-foot-high, intricately filigreed iron gate which was flanked with life-sized bronzed lions, poised to dispense with any and all undesirables.

Neither intimidated nor impressed, Sweetie growled and snarled at the statues. Only to have her style cramped by the very person she intended to protect.

Meanwhile, after fumbling in his pockets, Woody realized he had not been given any house keys.

"May I help you?" came a voice out of seemingly nowhere.

The accent was British. The gender male.

"May I help you?" repeated the voice.

"Ah, yeah, well, I hope so. I mean, I hope I've come to the

right place because otherwise I've just made a major ass of myself."

"Well, how will I ever be able to make this appraisal if you
don't reveal your identity, sir?"

"I guess you've got a point there. My name is Woody, well,
actually it's Clarence but I never use it and . . ."

Just like that, the gates opened.

Now, granted he'd seen many over-the-top homes on the
Key, but this one led the pack with its eclectic and comical
blend of architectural styles spanning centuries and countries.

The exterior walls were coquina, an off-white limestone
made out of crushed shells and coral.

Very roaring twenties Palm Beach.

The red-tiled roof evoked visions of an Italian Renaissance
palazzo.

The gilded double front door appeared to be fashioned after
those eighteenth century porte cocherés into which carriages
entered. So very Parisian.

And lining the driveway were a series of sculptures by
Columbian artist Fernando Botero. Morbidly obese naked women
in various poses, holding lit lanterns. Latin American contemporary hip.

Woody parked the car in front of this far from humble
home. No sooner had his flip-flops touched down upon the
blue-and-white delft-tiled pavement (very seventeenth century
Flemish), than Madalina bolted from the house. Clothed in a
slinky, short white silk bathrobe.

He nearly got a hard-on.

She leapt into his arms, wrapping her bare legs around him.
Kissing him over and over again.

This behavior, however, caused a certain four-legged female,
who was still seated in the car, to very vocally express her dis-
content. Her master apologized for his dog's behavior, but
Madalina appeared not to have cared.

"Oh, my God!" she squealed. She unhooked herself from Woody and ran over to the Porsche. "You have new car!"

"Ah, well, yeah, guess so. The Prince decided I needed something more suited for, well, my new lifestyle."

Those words fell out of his mouth so quickly it was scary.

"He make excellent choice for you, Voody."

"Not sure about that but what the hell. Must admit it's pretty cool driving. And my pooch, here, was totally into it. Speaking of whom, I ought to introduce you two."

He opened the door of the car, and the dog leapt out.

Sweetie stared at the "competition."

And the "competition" stared back at her.

Neither moved for a moment until the human broke down and made the first move.

"So you are famous Sweetie," said Madalina.

Woody tried not to be obvious, but when she leaned over, he caught a partial profile of her right bare breast.

"You are pretty dog, Sweetie."

Always a sucker for flattery, her tail began to wag like a metronome set to staccato.

"Yes, very, very pretty," she said, giving her a scratch behind her ears.

"I think she likes you. Don't you, girl?"

The dog smirked at her master as if to say, *I don't exactly have a choice in the matter, now do I?*

"Come, Voody. I must show you house. You not gonna believe your eyes."

They were greeted at the front door by the man he'd spoken to on the intercom. Reginald, the "butler." A middle-aged man attired in a morning suit, with nary a white hair on his head out of sync and posture straighter than a mast.

"Nice to meet you, Reginald. I'm Woody."

The butler neither smiled, nor frowned. "Let's say that's given, sir."

"Okay, I feel like a dork."

"That's hardly the case, sir."

This guy was unflappably polite.

"May I be of any more service tonight, sir?"

Woody laughed at the absurdity of the request.

"No, it's cool, thanks."

"Any special requests for breakfast, perhaps? I will leave a note for the cook."

"We have a cook?"

"Of course we do!" exclaimed Madalina. "Lots of servants. Is necessary for house like this."

And, as he was soon to learn, forty-five thousand square feet of pure materialistic decadence.

Madalina gave him the grand tour, highlighting some of her all-time favorite features:

The cavernous living room, its trompe l'oeil ceiling resembling a Louis XIV coronation room.

The ten-person screening room complete with commercial-sized popcorn machine and concession stand.

The professionally equipped kitchen with walk-in fireplace large enough, Woody joked, to roast a whole cow.

The dining room with its ornately carved table and twenty-four chairs covered in the finest Chinese silk.

The library with first edition classics lining the walls along with an Indian rosewood hand-carved pool table.

The infinity swimming pool with grotto waterfall and swim-up bar plus tennis court, gazebo and a dock suitable for tying up a fifty-foot boat.

Fifteen bedrooms.

Twenty bathrooms. The most amazing being large enough to accommodate a king and all his courtiers. It had a sunken Jacuzzi tub encircled by an indoor/outdoor garden over which hung cages filled with exotic birds.

Woody was amazed how at ease Madalina was as she strolled

from room to room. Especially since, by his calculations, she'd only just arrived at the house less than an hour prior to him.

Meanwhile, during this whirlwind tour, he realized Sweetie had somehow gone missing.

They found her in the master suite. Sprawled across the pillows of a gold leaf and inlaid pearl king-sized canopy bed.

Had the dog read his mind?

Chapter 21

For a fleeting moment, Woody thought the warm body next to his was Madalina's. But she was neither furry nor four-legged.

"Sure, you're all happy. Had me all to yourself last night, didn't you?"

Sweetie innocently rolled her eyes, licked his face and turned over for a belly rub. Canine victorious.

Unfortunately, Madalina, after teasing him to distraction, had shot down Woody once again. *Soon, soon,* she promised him. *We will make the love.*

Meanwhile, there was a knock at the door. Sweetie naturally responded to the intrusion.

"Voody?"

Warning his rambunctious pooch to behave, he swung his legs over the bed and sat up.

"Come on in!"

This morning, Madalina wore a pair of cut-off jeans and a white tank top with no bra underneath. Clothing designed to torture most unsuspecting young men.

"I see you are very happy to see me this morning," she said, giggling.

When Woody realized he had pitched a tent inside his boxers, he immediately doubled over and slipped back under the covers.

"Shit, sorry about that."

"You must not be sorry. Is means perhaps you were making sexy dreams of me, yes?"

"Always," he said, burying his head in his chest so deeply, the stubble of his unshaven chin nearly pierced his skin. "I think of you always. It's unavoidable. Can't help myself. I have this vision of you. Shit, never mind. Not even going to go there."

"You think of me naked?" asked Madalina, curling up next to him.

Woody swallowed a huge glob of saliva down the wrong tube and had a coughing fit.

She tenderly stroked his back. "You are okay?"

"Yeah, yeah. Fine."

"You are sure you must go to work? We could have much fun, I think."

The visuals of that notion made his head spin.

"Oh, man. I wish I didn't have to go."

"But is your day off."

"Skip's got to leave at ten-thirty. And he needs me there to cover."

"You know, Voody. Now that you have big fancy house, is silly to work at club."

"I, I can't quit my job. People count on me."

She climbed on top of him and nibbled on his earlobe.

"Stay with me, Voody," she whispered.

"Madalina—I can't believe I'm going to say this, but," he glanced at his watch. "Shit, it's already past eight! I really gotta go."

Chapter 22

Todd arrived at his parents' home severely hungover and sleep deprived.

His mother was still asleep—natch. The brat was primping herself for school, and his father was out on the terrace having a massage. The sight of Stanford's hirsute back always grossed him out. He wondered why, with all his money, his dad never got that disgusting shit lasered off. Perhaps beneath that macho bastard's exterior lurked the soul of a complete, pain phobic wimp.

Stanford looked up at him and pointed to a manila envelope sitting on one of his blue-and-white-striped designer chaise lounges. "It's over there."

No hello. Good morning. How are you, son?

"So, ah, Dad," said Todd. "How come I don't get to play golf with the big guys, too, this morning?"

"Not up for discussion. You do your job and I'll do mine. Now get your ass moving. Legal needs those papers at eight-thirty sharp."

"Fuck you very much," Todd mumbled to himself perhaps a dozen times as he traipsed through the house.

Anyway, he was just about to climb into his Hummer when he saw a brand-new black Porsche convertible pull out of the driveway across the street.

Todd squinted into the early morning sun and rubbed his eyes. The driver looked awfully familiar, but this made no sense.

Nor did the fact that Number Six Star Island Drive had been empty, in disrepair and tied up in probate court for four years.

He drove around to further investigate.

The rusted old gate and those wretched, chipped stone lions looked like new.

Weeds and dead trees had been substituted with beds of purple and white flowers and meticulously pruned vegetation.

Granted, Todd was so often wrapped up in his own world, he rarely noticed anything else, but he could have sworn this place looked nothing like this last week. Besides, if someone new had moved in, his parents would have surely made mention of it.

Todd's next stop was the guardhouse. Pierre would know the scoop. He had more dirt on everybody than a mountain's worth of landfill. But only at a price. He had kids in college to support.

"Yeah," said Pierre. "Guy moved in like overnight. Craziest damn thing."

"What's his name?" asked Todd.

"Woods," came the reply. "A Mr. Clarence W. Woods."

Chapter 23

"You're late," snapped Skip as Woody waltzed into the office.

"Sorry, boss. I completely overslept."

"You look like shit."

"Gee, thanks. And how are you feeling this morning?"

"Damn prostate kept me up all night. Maybe I should just sleep on the damn toilet."

"Now, that's an interesting visual. Sorry, boss, didn't mean to make light of your condition."

"It is what it is. One of the realities of a slowly decaying body. So what are you so damn perky about this morning? You and that waitress get it on or something?"

Before Woody could think of an evasive response, the phone rang.

"Who? Yeah, he's here. What? Hello? Son of a bitch!"

Skip slammed down the receiver with such force his coffee splashed over his desk.

"Rude prick hung up on me!"

"Who the hell was it?"

"No idea. But whoever it was seemed awfully interested in your whereabouts."

★ ★ ★

At precisely 10:17 A.M., the identity of the mystery caller was revealed.

Woody was in the middle of a friendly political debate with Misters Collier, Cox and Duke when Todd Hollings charged up the dock toward him.

"Hey, Woods!" he barked. "I need to talk to your ass!"

"Does that mean I need to bend over?"

All three members of the Geezer Patrol found this remark humorous. Not so with young Hollings.

"You've got some major explaining to do."

"Really?" asked Woody. "Mind clueing me in on what?"

"I was at my parents' this morning, and I saw you coming out of the Dawson estate. Driving a Porsche, no less."

A lump the size of a grenade formed in Woody's throat. He had no idea the Hollings clan lived on Star Island. No wonder Madalina had been so intent upon moving there. Still, he had to admit the payoff was, in a sick kind of way, brilliant.

"Why should you care?" asked Woody.

"For starters, nobody has lived there for years."

"What makes you think I do?"

"Don't play me for a fool, douche bag. You're listed as the owner."

"That so?"

Woody never expected screwing with this asshole's head would be so much fun.

"How's this possible?" asked Todd.

"Well, Miami is known as the magic city, so maybe I just got real lucky, huh?"

"Bullshit! There's no way you could ever make that kind of money. You're nothing but a slacker. A loser. Pushing thirty and still working as a dock boy."

And just like that, without thinking twice, peace-loving, gentle Woody delivered a swift, hard punch to Todd Hollings's right cheek. The boy stumbled back, and in a most ungraceful manner, lost his balance and fell into the water.

Cussing and sputtering, Todd swam to the ladder and climbed back up onto the dock. His clothes plastered to his body and minus one of his shoes and his sunglasses.

"You are so fucking busted!"

Todd lunged for Woody, but his leather-soled loafer went out from under him, and he landed, hard, on his well-toned gluteus maximus.

Much to the sadistic delight of the Geezer Patrol.

Skip bounded out of the office and plunked his six-four frame—a little timeworn but still imposing—in the middle of the tempest.

"What the hell's going on here?"

Mr. Cox stepped forward. "A very heated altercation obviously."

"Woody delivered a right hook," piped in Mr. Duke. "Damn good one at that."

Skip looked at him in disbelief. "You started this?"

"He provoked me," said Woody.

Todd rose to his feet. He vigorously brushed himself off as if to iron out the wrinkles in his now-shrunken suit.

"I need you to fire him right now," he sneered.

"Whoa," said Skip. "There's no need for such a drastic move. I'm sure it was just a minor misunderstanding."

"Sure didn't sound like it to us," said Mr. Duke. "Right, boys?"

The other members of the Geezer Patrol nodded in agreement.

"Gentlemen," said Skip. "I'd appreciate it if you kept your opinions to yourselves and let me handle this. Now, where were we?"

"You were going to fire Woody," said Todd. "Because if you don't, my father will have his job and yours!"

"That's right, Hollings," said Woody. "Let Daddy make it all better. Just like he tried to get my aunt fired when she flunked you in biology."

"Ugly old cunt had it coming to her."

As this affront could not go unpunished, Woody took another swing at Todd. He ducked out of the way but, unfortunately, his boss took the brunt of the hit.

Skip rubbed his jaw. "You pack quite a punch, son."

"So sorry about that, boss. You all right?"

"Yeah, fine. Don't worry about it, son. Kind of takes me back to all those barroom brawls I had when I was in the navy."

"Why don't you ask your stellar employee here what he's doing living in a mansion on Star Island?" shouted Todd, keeping a safe distance. "Because I'm sure Miami PD would be interested in hearing his explanation as well."

Heads turned and mouths dropped.

"Star Island?" Skip and the Geezer Patrol exclaimed in unison.

"Maybe the kid is dealing drugs," said Mr. Duke.

"Got to be serious drugs to live there," repeated Mr. Collier.

"If I were doing that," said Woody. "Would I be still busting my butt here?"

With all eyes and ears on him, Woody suddenly felt boxed into a corner from which he knew there was only one means of escape.

Chapter 24

His head awhirl after his impromptu resignation, Woody jumped into the Porsche and headed straight for the Cape Florida Lighthouse.

Located in Bill Baggs Park at the southernmost tip of Key Biscayne, this ninety-five-foot-tall historic landmark was a refuge to which he and his uncle had occasionally retreated. They would gaze at the panoramic view of the Atlantic Ocean and inevitably find themselves daydreaming about adventures they'd like to take. It had been six years since the last time Woody had set foot in the tower. The day his uncle Herb passed away.

Woody raced up the one hundred and nineteen spiraling iron steps and didn't stop until he reached the lantern room. Although the skies were a bit overcast, the aquamarine water never looked so seductive. In fact, had the *Sea Sponge* been ready, he just might have set sail that very afternoon.

Technicalities aside, however, life just wasn't as simple anymore.

He was head over heels in love.

The moment Woody burst through the French doors to the veranda, Sweetie ran to him as if he'd been gone for an eternity.

Madalina, however, was fast asleep, floating on a raft in the middle of the pool. Wearing a tiny red bikini and appearing even more beautiful than she had when he left her earlier that morning. His first instinct was to tear off his clothes and dive in after her, but he knew this wasn't an option. Wouldn't want to give the girl a major fright.

Resigned to wait as long as it took—the view, after all, couldn't have been more appealing—Woody pulled a chaise lounge up to the water's edge. The moment he sat down, however, Madalina's eyes popped open.

"Oh, my God!" she gasped.

"I didn't mean to scare you."

"I was sleeping so sound. What is time, Voody?"

"Eleven-thirty."

"You have come home so early?"

Woody focused his attention on an ant dragging a crumb twice its size across the ground.

"I, I quit my job this morning."

Madalina squealed and bounded off the raft. Dripping wet, she jumped into his lap and threw her arms around him.

"But is great news!"

"Not so sure about that."

"You must tell me what happened."

Woody filled her in on the details. Her favorite part being when Todd fell into the water.

"Oh, I wish I have seen this!"

"Guess it was pretty comical," he said stoically.

"But why you still look so sad? Be happy you are now free."

But for what price?

Outside of a couple of college internships, working at the Trade Winds Yacht Club was the only job he'd ever known.

"I have great idea to make you feel better . . ."

Woody secretly wished she had plans for them to spend the

rest of the afternoon and evening—oh, hell, perhaps the rest of the week!—in bed.

"You must have how they call, 'retail therapy.'"

"I assume that involves spending money and . . ."

Woody began to laugh.

"What is funny?"

"Just look around us. We're living like royalty, and I have, well. exactly three hundred and forty dollars in the bank . . ."

He stopped midsentence.

"Holy shit. I totally forgot."

"Forgot what?"

"This," said Woody.

He laid open the wallet Raymond had given him and handed it to Madalina. Her pupils dilated with the intensity of a supernova as she pulled out the black credit card.

"I have read about Centurion American Express card in *Fortune*."

"You read that magazine?"

"Of course. Doesn't everybody?"

With the ease of a veteran sailor, Madalina cruised from one end of the Bal Harbour mall to the other, stopping at several ports of call along the way to barter for goods with the natives.

"Two hundred and fifty dollars for jeans? Forty-five dollars for plaid boxers? One hundred dollars for a white T-shirt? You must be kidding."

Speaking as one who still favored his high school vintage ensembles, little wonder Woody was aghast. Nonetheless, his personal stylist—armed with *GQ* and *Men's Vogue*—was determined to update his wardrobe.

"After the first thousand dollars, it will get easier," Madalina assured him.

"I'm still not comfortable with this."

"Retail therapy must make you feel good, not bad."

The reluctant shopper frowned at his reflection in the mirror. *Who is this alien,* he thought. With these tight, uncomfortable clothes he looked like every other slick Miami hipster.

"Want to know what makes me feel good, no, great? It's being with you. Not blowing cash on shit I don't need."

"My sweet, silly Voody."

She rose to her toes and planted a wet, sensual kiss to his lips and then promptly handed him a Ralph Lauren Purple Label blue blazer and a pair of linen pants.

"Of course, you need."

Two hours later, Woody called for an embargo on men's clothes. Although convinced these purchases were superfluous, he kept his opinions to himself. No need to hurt Madalina's feelings after she'd worked so diligently to give him a "new look."

"Okay, now it's your turn," he said, handing over the credit card to Madalina.

"Really?"

"Would I lie to you?"

While Madalina ran off on her treasure hunt, Woody parked his bones in an easy chair. Who could have imagined retail therapy would be such an aerobic workout? As for the mood-elevation part, well, he'd been so busy spending money, there was no time left to focus on the negative. In fact, Woody had just begun to nod off when he felt someone's face practically in his. Someone who'd (a) recently eaten onions and (b) doused themselves with a gallon of cologne.

"Woody? Is that you?"

The voice was male. The intonation nasal. Woody opened his eyes.

"Mr. Sage."

It had been exactly one week since the last time he'd seen the captain of the *Midas Touch*. Today, he was hard to miss. He was wearing a yellow track suit so bright, he could be spotted from several miles away. His jacket was unzipped halfway down his chest, exposing an enormous golden crucifix and decidedly a lot more hair than what was on his head.

"Fred. Call me Fred."

He inspected the bags surrounding Woody and nodded his head.

"Lauren, Prada. Professionally speaking, I'd say someone's bank account has sustained serious friggin' damage today."

Woody suddenly felt the impact of his battle wounds and sunk even deeper into the chair.

"Seems like your money problems must have been solved, huh, kid? Now I don't feel bad stiffing you."

"So, ah, how are you feeling, uh, Fred?" asked Woody, changing the subject.

"Me? Fit as a friggin' fiddle. Why do you ask?"

"You weren't doing so well last time I saw you."

Fred shook his head. "Don't remind me. As we speak, I'm trying to unload that frickin' boat. You've probably been wondering why I haven't been around Trade Winds."

Not exactly, thought Woody. He also didn't feel it necessary to divulge the fact he was no longer employed at the club.

"Got into a bit of trouble with my honey," he said. "And here she comes right now."

Fred's fiancée, decked out in a bright pink velour jacket, hot pants and rhinestone-encrusted sneakers, sauntered up to them. Fred reached out and drew her to him.

"I just love, love, love my baby!" he exclaimed, kissing her cheek.

Trish blew a bubble the size of her head and popped it. "Yech," she said, wiggling loose from her fiancé. "Your breath still stinks from lunch."

"Remember Woody from the club, honey bunny?"

"Let's not even, like, you know, go there. No offense," she said, addressing Woody. "But it's like a real sore subject with me."

"Don't worry about it. It's cool."

"The truth is," said Fred. "It took me a week to get out of the doghouse. Only reason the warden here decided to let me out today is because I bribed her with a trip to Neiman Marcus. Right, honey bunny?"

"Damn straight and, pops, is it ever going to cost you!"

In the midst of this intellectually vapid conversation, Madalina emerged from the fitting room clad in a tasteful, body-hugging black shift.

"You look incredible," said Woody, trying to catch his breath.

She spun around like a supermodel. "So you like?"

"I'll say."

"Is Gucci."

Woody nodded his head in recognition, but it was bullshit. Sure, he could rattle off the names and longitudes of all the major ports in the world or discuss the merits of one nautical architect versus another with expert authority. But query him on the simplest fashion question and he'd fail miserably.

Fred leered at her. "So who is this lovely lady with wickedly expensive taste?"

"Sorry, that was rude of me," said Woody. "Mr. Sage. Trish. This is Madalina, my, my . . ."

"Girlfriend," she said, completing his sentence. "Is nice to meet you."

Holy shit, thought Woody, still reeling from the impact of this newly acquired title.

"Cute accent," said Trish. "Where you all from?"

"I am Romanian."

"Really? My cousin, Dino, he's from Italy, too."

Fred leaned toward Woody and nudged his shoulder.

"Va-va-voomski with the dish."

"Stick your tongue back in your mouth," said Trish, smacking Fred with her handbag. "It's rude! Men are such animals, but as long as they supply the goods, I guess we can put up with them, right, 'Lina?"

"What this means?" asked Madalina.

"It means that we girls need to look at love as a matter of business. If money doesn't talk, honey, we walk!"

"After all the cash I just dropped, I don't know whether I should slit my wrists or go drown myself in food and wine," declared Fred. "What say we all head over to the local cantina?"

Before Woody could conjure up an excuse to bail, Trish and Madalina, who'd suddenly become "best friends," were all over his proposal.

"We should go to La Gouloue," said Madalina, with perfect enunciation.

"Yeah, Le Goolie," piped in Trish. "The place to see and be seen for sure. And it's right here in the Bal Harbour mall."

Although pretty much anything went when it came to dress code in Miami, the maitre d' at the posh restaurant nonetheless copped a 'tude when this party of four arrived. The restaurant was still pretty empty, but sadly, all he could offer at this time was a table right next to the kitchen.

Fred opined loud enough for the entire restaurant to hear. "What a bunch of bullshit."

"We don't care," insisted Trish. "We still want to stay, right, 'Lina?"

"Is okay, Voody?"

One look from those eyes was all he needed in order to drink the Kool–Aid.

"Damn frog," mumbled Fred as he watched the maitre d' prance off. "Look at the way he walks. Betcha anything he takes it up the ass."

Meanwhile, what Fred lacked in social graces, he made up for with a sophisticated choice in wine.

"We need a bottle of this," he said, pointing to an item on the list.

"Moulin Touchais Coteaux du Layon, 1971? Excellent choice, monsieur," said the sommelier.

"It ought to be at three hundred bucks a pop!"

"Wine is Fred's hobby," said Trish. "Ever since he took this course, the man is totally obsessed. Built a special wine cellar and everything."

"We have many, many bottles, too, in our house," said Madalina.

Trish turned to her fiancé. "They just moved into a mansion on Star Island, for your information."

Personally, Woody wasn't keen on having this fact broadcast to the general public. What he had acquired wasn't illegal, but it was certainly illogical.

"Damn, boy," exclaimed Fred. "What did you do? Find a genie in a magic lantern?"

"In a manner of speaking, I guess so," said Woody, nervously chortling.

"So, give us the scoop," said Trish.

"It's quite a tale," said Woody, blinking at Madalina.

Enlisting all his creative powers, Woody fabricated a story about a great-uncle, "Ray," who, after making his millions in building retirement homes in the southwest, married his recently widowed high school sweetheart after fifty years of confirmed bachelorhood.

"Wow," said Trish, sighing. "How romantic! Then what happened?"

"My uncle Ray, ah, Raymond, well, he bought the house on Star Island for them as a wedding gift. Had it completely furnished and stuff."

"But why didn't they move in?"

"Honey bunny, stop beating those cute little gums of yours and let the kid finish."

"Well, it's pretty tragic, actually, because on their honeymoon in Bali they decided to go snorkeling. I'm afraid their bodies were never recovered."

"Jesus," said Fred. "Well, at least they didn't grow to hate each other."

Trish shoved her fiancé. "It's not funny. It's sad. Actually, I think I read about them in *People* or something."

Woody looked over at Madalina, who was biting her nails in what appeared to be a concerted effort to keep from losing it. As laughter can be most infectious, he did his best to maintain composure.

"Anyway, I'm my uncle's sole heir, and the will was read just last week."

Trish's brown eyes turned bright green. "What a catch you've got yourself, 'Lina. Lucky you!"

"Yes, I am very lucky girl to find my Voody."

"Where on earth did you guys meet?"

"At Trade Winds Yacht Club."

"You're a member?" asked Fred.

"No, no, a waitress."

"A former waitress," said Woody.

"Really? Is true?" whispered Madalina.

"Would I lie to you?"

And with that, in a very enthusiastic public display of affection, she gave Woody a full-mouthed, sustained kiss.

"Aw," said Trish. "How sweet."

"What about you, kid?" asked Fred. "You going to quit, too?"

"I basically took care of that this morning."

"Smart move but I gotta tell you, what with all these new assets, you got to start sinking some of that cash into real estate. It's where it's all happening here in South Florida."

Chapter 25

The loss of Todd's hard-on almost came as no surprise. It was just a crowning moment in a chain reaction of mishaps originating that morning at the yacht club.

The Prada suit. Trashed.

The Gucci alligator loafer. Missing.

His favorite shades. Gone.

His BlackBerry. Rendered inoperable.

And how about that shiner below his right eye?

But alas, the fun had just started.

While driving on Brickell, a half-blind grandma cut him off. Swerving to avoid her, Todd rammed into a Ford Taurus exiting the Four Seasons Hotel. The driver spoke no English, which came as no surprise to Todd as this problem afflicted more than half of the population of Miami.

"I need to call the police to make a report," he said. "You understand? *Policia.*"

"*Näo, Näo! Näo policias!*" he shrieked in Portuguese.

And with that, the man ran, screaming, to his car and slammed his body inside. He promptly drove away. Dragging behind his fender and dented trunk.

Todd's Hummer barely sustained a scratch; however, his right front wheel had taken the brunt of the impact and was flat. As he lacked the skills with which to change the tire, he intended to dial up "Triple A," when he remembered this was an impossible feat.

"Fuck!" he screamed, jettisoning his useless mobile phone across the tarmac.

The next option was to flag down someone to help. A task as difficult as, say, finding a girl in South Beach who won't put out on the first date.

A half hour later, a middle-aged salesman from Milwaukee finally stopped to assist. Todd offered him a hundred spot, but the guy refused the money. Seemed he was more interested in oral compensation. Needless to say, Todd was back on the road faster than you could say "homo."

He did manage to get to his apartment without further incident; however, traipsing through his lobby in a crumpled suit, no shoes and a black eye was embarrassing to say the least.

After a quick shower and change of clothes, Todd patronized his favorite boutique on Lincoln Road before heading to the office. He bought a new pair of shades and also met a totally hot girl named Darlene. After winning her sympathy vote (with his cockamamie story about a "damsel in distress"), he got her to agree to hook up with him later that night for dinner and clubbing, which he hoped to leverage into more.

Then, of course, his BlackBerry had to be replaced and, even though the phone was only three months old, he just had to upgrade. More time wasted on account of slow help.

Todd finally arrived at the office—at exactly 2:32 P.M.—only to learn he'd missed his appointment with Mr. Gustavo Tinnie—the key contact in the Virginia Key deal. He didn't even want to think how his father would react to this royal fuck-up, so he needed a little diversionary Internet surfing.

This decision proved to be a bad choice when his monitor froze on a photo of a blond midget having "every hole plugged" by a trio of African-Americans with monster dicks. Todd had no choice but to call the I.T. department, who promptly dispatched a newly hired techie—one William Silver—who happened to be a former high school classmate of Todd's. Specifically, a geek whom he and the other jocks used to torment every chance they got.

By day's end, everybody in the company would know what a pervert the boss's son was.

But the fun was far from finished.

Todd spilled iced latte over an original set of architectural plans.

Lindsay, his coed girlfriend up north, called to inform him her period was late.

His father was on his way to the office. And from what Todd's secretary could gather, he did not sound very happy.

"What are you, incognito? Take off those damn sunglasses!"

Todd reluctantly complied with his father's wishes.

"What the hell happened to your eye?"

"Got into a fight."

"Who in the world with? Minnie Mouse?"

"Woody. You know, the dock boy from—"

"Trade Winds? Never would have pegged him as confrontational. Kid has such a gentle soul. You must have really done something to piss him off."

It was so typical of his father to endorse the enemy and convict his kin before all the evidence had been presented.

"But you don't understand, Dad. It's, well, complicated."

"What do you take me for, some kind of idiot?"

Todd figured he might as well just blurt it out.

"Woody just bought an estate on Star Island. In fact, the Dawson house across the road."

His father stared long and hard at him. "Philip's place? How the hell is that possible?"

"Precisely my question."

Chapter 26

Upon learning of Madalina's plans for them to spend the morning at some fancy spa, Woody politely tried to bail. But after being groomed, wrapped in seaweed and massaged for ninety minutes, there was no denying how relaxed he felt. Madalina had also made lunch reservations at La Piaggia—yet another "trendy" South Beach eatery about which she'd read in one of her rags.

Woody rather liked the restaurant's beachfront ambiance with its sandy floor, yellow-and-white-striped banquettes and bright orange umbrellas. But he could have done without the self-indulgent, self-centered, predominantly Euro crowd, many of whom were in various stages of undress.

Not so with Madalina. She couldn't stop people watching. Within minutes of being seated she'd spied Lindsay Lohan, Nicholas Cage and P. Diddy plus entourage.

"Look who was just seated! Is Mr. Trump. But wait. Who is this man with him? I have seen him before, I am sure."

Woody subtly peeked over his shoulder. He identified the mystery diner immediately by his bioengineered hair and teeth.

"Hmm," he said, grunting. "That's Stanford Hollings."

"You mean father of Todd?"

It tickled him that she still mispronounced that asshole's name.

"Phooey," she said, pretending to spit. "I have great dislike for him. He is big asshole shit like son. Why would The Donald—*Doodled*—eat with person like this?"

"Maybe they're friends, Madalina."

"Or maybe they make big real estate deal together. I remember Todd says his father build big buildings."

"Yes, he does. All over the frickin' place."

Madalina took a large swig of Rose and repositioned the crab cake on her plate.

"You know, Voody, perhaps you should think about new career."

"Doing what, is the big question. I can just see the story in the tabloids," he said, chuckling. "Guy slings burgers at McDonald's by day. Lives in multimillion-dollar-mansion by night. Makes for interesting copy, huh?"

"Is not funny, Voody. You must not be happy to just make good living. You must, like Mr. Trump says, make big statement. Because if you and me, we are to be married—"

"Whoa," he said, interrupting. "Hold on. Did, did you just say married?"

Granted, the concept was way premature, but then again, his Aunt Katherine and Herb got hitched a month after meeting. And until the day he died, those two were totally devoted to each other.

Madalina played with her lower lip. "I thought you loved me, Voody."

"Yes, I do. Very much."

"And I love you too."

"You do?"

Woody knew he'd been living in a fantasy world for the past week or so, but man, he hoped Madalina was being sincere.

"Of course, silly boy. I am big, big crazy for you!"

He had this sudden urge to jump across the table and pull her underneath. But he naturally controlled himself.

"At the risk of sounding really sappy, I must confess. You have no idea how you've changed my life."

All the material possessions excluded.

"And is good?"

"Is wonderful."

"We can make even better, I think."

"How?"

Please say sex, thought Woody.

"You must go back to fish," she said, without blinking an eye.

"For, for what reason?"

"You must tell Prince you want to be real estate developer, too. Like Mr. Trump. Only much much bigger."

"But why?"

"To really piss off father of Todd Hollings."

"Madalina, I don't think I can really ask Raymond for such a thing."

"Of course you can. You can do anything you want."

She pulled her chair close to Woody's and slowly guided her fingers under his shorts. In five seconds, the last remnants of the poor boy's willpower dribbled onto his plate of dorade royale.

Chapter 27

"You scared the be-Jesus out of me" exclaimed Katherine nearly spilling her green tea over the kitchen table. "Didn't hear you come in, sugar."

"Little wonder that," said Woody, muting the 6:00 o'clock news.

She watched him mosey on over to the fridge and pour himself a glass of chocolate milk. Aside from one quick phone call, Woody had been out of communication with her for nearly forty-eight hours.

"Will you please stop staring at me like I'm some kind of alien?"

"What's different about you?"

"I, uh, had my hair styled."

Sure enough, that mane had been tamed and trimmed by someone other than a blind one-armed gardener with a weed-whacker.

"Back where I come from we call that a haircut. But there's something else. It's your clothes. Are they new?"

"As a matter of fact, yeah, they are."

Gone were the baggy, thread-bare shorts customarily splattered with paint, stain, varnish or the like. Missing was the loose

T-shirt—white or dirty white—and the ten-year-old Teva flip-flops.

They were replaced by the following:

One pair of tan linen Bermudas—tailored and alligator-belted.

One blue-and-white-striped button-down shirt with embroidered polo player—tail tucked into pants.

One orange cotton sweater also with embroidered polo player—worn over shoulders.

One pair of moccasins adorned with a light gold horse bit—no socks.

Katherine patted her bottom lip with an index finger several times and then spoke.

"You all certainly look terrific, but sugar, come on. I can't remember the last time you bought something new. Let alone something that was not from the Salvation Army store. Besides, since when did you start making a fuss over something other than that boat of yours?"

"Well, maybe . . ."

Woody excavated a corner of his head, twiddled whatever it was he'd found between his fingers and then flicked it away.

". . . Maybe that was part of my problem."

Although perhaps true, this admission was nonetheless severely out of character.

"Come sit down here with your old auntie for a sec, sugar. You got something you'd like to tell me?"

"Like what?" he asked, his voice elevating several octaves.

"For starters, when you and your canine co-conspirator failed to come home last night from wherever you were, naturally this gave me pause . . ."

He rolled his eyes and played a drum roll on the table.

". . . And I know it's none of my business where you go or who you all are with."

"No shit!"

"Don't you sass-ass me, Clarence."

He lowered his chin and mumbled he was sorry.

"Anyway, on the morning news, I heard about this god-awful accident over on Rickenbacker, and I got a bit frantic because there was no way to get in touch with you to make sure you were all right. I mean, I don't care where you go, but . . ."

"Here," said Woody, interrupting.

He scribbled on a piece of paper and handed it to Katherine. She, in turn, gazed at the numerals as if they had been written by an orangutan. That boy always had the worst handwriting.

"Is this a seven or a one?"

"A one.

"Whose number is this?"

"Mine. It's my cell phone number. Now you can always reach me if you have to."

Katherine shook her head. "Excuse me, but aren't you the same person who swore he'd never get one of those contraptions?"

"A cell phone, I've found, has some major advantages."

"Hmm. I see. Anyway, like I was saying, I got real worried this morning, so I called the Trade Winds."

Her nephew's eyes darted from side to side and he scratched his neck. Katherine knew his body language all too well. The question was, would he come clean?

"Y-y-you spoke to Skip?"

"No, he wasn't there, but Mary at the front desk told me you up and quit.

"I got a better offer, that's all."

Katherine was about to ask what the hell that was when Sweetie started to bark, and then ran off towards the front door.

"Expecting company?" asked Woody.

"I asked Dorothy to pick up a Big Bang lottery ticket for me."

Katherine's friend walked into the kitchen. She seemed taken aback when she saw Woody.

"Is that your Porsche parked out front?"

"Ah, yeah. Sort of."

His aunt whipped round her head so quickly her levator scapulae muscle failed to engage, causing a pain to shoot through her neck.

"Did I just hear right?"

"I had to bring the pickup to the shop, and a woman from the club loaned me her car."

Katherine and Dorothy exchanged glances and then ogled Woody.

"She's got a whole bunch," he said. "Four. No, actually, five. You know how these rich people like to collect stuff. Anyway, um, she asked me to pet-sit for her while she goes off to Europe for an extended visit."

"Pet-sit, huh?" asked Katherine.

"Yeah, you should see these dogs. Great Danes, Harlequins. She's going to pay me a salary. Actually, more money than I got at the club."

"Who is this woman?"

"Mrs. Nascinento," said Woody. "Her name is Mrs. Nascinento. She's, ah, Brazilian. Filthy rich."

It amazed Woody how quickly he was able to fabricate a story. And how little guilt he felt telling it.

"I still don't understand the bit about the sports car."

"She, uhm, insisted. It belonged to her late husband. Her ex, that is. She doesn't speak very highly of the dude, so he must have really pissed her off. So I figured, hey, I've never driven in a Porsche before, so you know, now is as good a time as ever. Right?"

"Why the hell not," said Dorothy, who seemed to have

bought the bullshit Woody had just sold. "I sure as hell would have done the same thing were I you."

"Yeah, because you're an old whore," said Katherine.

"Better than a cheapskate," piped in Dorothy.

"Ladies, ladies," said Woody. "Be nice."

Katherine shot a finger at her friend and continued.

"So let me get this straight. You quit your job, a job that you loved for so many years, in order to work for this woman."

"Yep! And the good news is I'll have more time to spend on the *Sponge*. Who knows, maybe I'll finish her ahead of schedule."

"Where does this broad live?" asked Dorothy.

"Star Island."

"Whoa. Serious money over there."

"Yeah, guess so. Anyway, that's where I've, ah, been the past several nights. For a kind of dry run. You know, just to make sure I know where everything in the house is and stuff, and that Sweetie and Mrs. Nascinento's dogs could, you know, get along okay."

Katherine wanted to delve deeper into the dung heap that had piled up in her kitchen, but Woody's cell phone started to ring. Or rather played a tune. Specifically, a song that Katherine recognized from the sixties.

"Do you believe in magic?" the ladies exclaimed together.

"The Mamas and the Papas," shouted Dorothy, determined to beat her friend to the answer.

"No way," said Katherine. "The Lovin' Spoonful. I used to have a mad crush on John Sebastian."

"Excuse me, but I gotta take this call," said Woody, scurrying out of the kitchen.

Katherine turned to Dorothy when her nephew was safely out of ear range and whispered, "There's no doubt in my mind now. That boy has taken up with an older woman."

"Never pegged him for boy toy material."

"I think I feel sick."

"Come on, Katherine. These days, it's quite in vogue to have a young lover. Maybe I should get me one of those."

"Oh, shut up, Dorothy. Something smells awfully fishy to me."

Chapter 28

"Dorothy split already?" asked Woody, returning to the kitchen. His chat with Madalina had been long enough for her to remind him of the importance of his "mission" and then, of course, tell him how much she loved him.

"She was late for bingo," said Katherine.

"What say I take you out to celebrate my new job?"

She balked at the idea of patronizing "some damn overpriced, overcrowded tourist joint" where the food was sure to be inferior to hers, but Woody was able to convince Katherine of the merits of having one of Archie's gourmet pizzas—with pepperoni and mushrooms—delivered.

Thanks to a couple of Bloody Marys, Katherine was in rare form. Dispensing with any further interrogation, she reminisced about some of the old days on Key Biscayne. Classic stories Woody had heard before, but of which he never tired. Like the anti-Vietnam War protest Katherine organized outside former President Nixon's "Winter White House" on Harbor Drive and how Tricky Dick had milk and cookies sent out in an attempt to appease the rowdy pacifists. Or, one of Woody's favorites about the infamous Quarterdeck Club in Stiltsville. Before the place burnt down in '61, Katherine and Herb often motored out to this unique spot out on the water. Thanks to the potholes located underneath each bar stool, customers could drop a line and fish while they got sauced up. Katherine and Herb were there the night Rufus Knowles, the Quarterdeck Club's resident drunk, actually hooked himself a blue shark which nearly cost the bastard both testicles!

Woody couldn't remember the last time he'd spent more than fifteen minutes at the table. The excuse of working on the *Sea Sponge* certainly had merit, but there was more to this behavior.

Aside from sailing, the absence of Woody's late uncle Herb was felt the most at dinner.

Herb, armed with a martini, would always hold court at the table. Whether it was just the three of them or invited guests, the conversation was always stimulating. The subject matter diverse. The debates sometimes heated. And the laughter—like the quality of Katherine's cooking—always guaranteed.

Now Woody told his aunt, "Just couldn't pull myself away from the pleasure of your company."

"You're full of shit sometimes, but I do love you, sugar."

He leaned over and planted a kiss on her cheek. "The feelings are mutual."

Katherine yawned. "Good, now that that's settled, I think it's time for this old broad to head for bed."

Woody pulled on his sweater and headed outside.

Thanks to a fast-moving high pressure system from the northeast (still digging out from a blizzard) the temperature had dropped to fifty-six degrees, near bone-chilling to many a native Floridian. And given the predominance of whitecaps which had pockmarked Biscayne Bay, the winds had to be blowing some twenty to thirty knots.

Woody chose not to sit on the seawall. He didn't want to mess up his new clothes—a ludicrous decision considering his former slovenly ways.

"Here goes nothing," he said out loud.

Despite his second thoughts concerning Madalina's latest list of demands, he couldn't bring himself to let her down, so once again he summoned Raymond Prince with his banjo.

But the fish was a no show.

Perhaps the required notes of "Foggy Mountain Breakdown" had gotten lost in the din, he thought and played the tune again.

Still not a peep from his aquatic amigo.

Two more encores followed one after the other.

Woody surveyed the area with his flashlight. "RAYMOND? ARE YOU THERE?"

Nothing. Nada. Nunka.

"Maybe it's just as well Raymond didn't show," he said to his dog. "I mean, I'm in this whole thing way, way over my head. But you know what's really fucked up?"

Sweetie cocked her head as if to say: *like you don't know already?*

"I'm actually going to miss our little talks." Woody packed away his banjo in the case. "Come on, girl. Let's go break the news to Madalina."

"HEY!" shouted a voice. "Where the hell do you think you're going?"

Woody turned around so quickly, he nearly knocked his dog into the water.

"Raymond! Am I ever glad to see you!"

"Face it. You just love me for my money."

"Nah," said Woody, laughing. "But it sure enriches the relationship. Seriously, though, when you didn't show up I got real worried. Thought something happened to you."

The fish tried to steady himself in the surf, a none-too-easy task given the conditions that night.

"You have no idea what I went through to get here. It'd make traffic on I–95 during rush hour seem like the Indianapolis 500 in comparison. I hit one wall after another. First it was this school of red snappers. Then Spanish mackerel. Followed by all these damn pompanos who just wouldn't get out of my way because the females were busy dropping all their eggs and shit. Talk about losing your erection. Disgusting. Anyway, I decided to take a detour into let's just say the wrong 'hood. Damn sharks all over the place. Checking me out like I was a prime rib special! Let me tell you, I got the hell out of there as fast as my ass, er, tail could carry me. Unfortunately, in my posthaste, I managed to overshoot my exit."

"Excuse my ignorance, but how do you determine where that is?"

"Simple. When you get to this sunken trawler some schmuck actually named *Ship-faced,* you take a right into the reefs and then another left. I had to backtrack and, what with these wicked currents, I nearly got stuck in lobster trap line. Anyway, that's all in my rearview mirror now, and here I am. At your service."

The fish scanned Woody from top to bottom.

"Hmm, looks like somebody got a makeover. This is a great look for you, kid."

"Madalina was my own personal shopper, actually."

"I kind of figured that black Am Ex would come in handy. How is the little lady, by the way?"

"She's amazing."

"No doubt happy with the Star Island crib?"

"I'll say."

"You happy with the Porsche?"

"Yeah, thanks. It's quite the driving machine."

"So I assume by now you're having mind-blowing sex, right?"

Woody nibbled on a nail. "Well, we've been, ah, well, you know, real close."

He refused to tell him about the skinny dipping episode in the pool the previous night. About Madalina swimming up behind him and biting him on the ass. Or about the flesh-to-flesh embrace followed by deep, prolonged kissing where Woody's level of excitement shot from Guarded to Elevated to High and finally Code Red Severe until, despite all efforts to counter the situation, his defense system failed, and he shot his wad into the chlorinated water. He'd never been more embarrassed.

"Close, you say," said Raymond, snickering. "Hell, in my book, close is only good for horseshoes and hand grenades. But I gotta tell you, this is one crafty girl. Certainly is an expert at using the promise of sex to keep you dangling, eh?"

"It's going to happen soon. She's just not ready to consummate our relationship yet."

"Uh-huh."

"Hey, I do have some progress to report. Major progress actually. Madalina and I are talking m-m-marriage."

The verb had not quite yet fit into his vocabulary.

"Should I congratulate you or offer my condolences?"

"Stop being so cynical."

"You gotta understand where I'm coming from here, kid. This fucking curse my wife slapped on me doesn't exactly make for a good attitude toward the, ah, blessed union, if you know what I mean."

"Speaking of which, the moon's about to be full again soon."

"Believe me, kid, I'm fully aware of that fact."

"Have you found out a way to reverse this spell yet?"

"Let me put it this way. I'm swimming in the right direction." The Prince took a beat and then smiled. "So the bottom line is, what can I do you for tonight, kid?"

"Well, to be honest—"

"No," said the Prince, interrupting. "Lie to me."

"Madalina thinks I need a job."

"What happened to the one at the yacht club?"

"I quit."

"Smart move."

"Not sure about that. But meanwhile, we were having lunch today at La Piaggia . . ."

"Plenty of movers and shakers at that joint."

"That explains seeing Trump, I guess."

"The Donald apparently loves the food."

"He was with Stanford Hollings."

"Talking shop, no doubt."

"Who knows, but Madalina got this crazy idea in her head that I should get into real estate."

"Real estate, huh?"

Woody braced for the Prince's reaction.

"I love it! I just love it!"

"You do?"

"The girl is genius. It's like the perfect revenge. Man, seeing the expression on Hollings' face when we hit him right between his dollars and cents would be worth seeing."

"So you can actually pull this off? This is a pretty tall order and all and . . ."

"Hey," said Raymond interrupting. "Of course, the Prince can make you a deal you won't forget. All you have to do is A-S-K."

"Yes, yes. Let's make this happen."

"Kid, you've got yourself a deal! Run home to Madalina and give her the good news."

"Thanks, Raymond! I owe you big for this one!"

"Believe me, the pleasure, my friend, will soon be all mine."

And with that a crest of cappuccino-like froth rose higher and higher around the fish's body until the water swallowed him up.

Woody found three items waiting for him on the front seat of the Porsche:

1. A little blue box from Tiffany in which was a ten-carat surprise.
2. A large black briefcase stuffed with documents in which Woody had no interest.
3. A note:

Remember the art of the deal.
Don't close until you see the white of their checkbooks.
The Prince.

Chapter 29

Woody neglected to notice a collection of newly posted billboards along the route back to Star Island. Each fifteen-by-forty-eight-foot canvas depicted Frank Gehry–designed apartment towers slated for waterfront construction throughout the greater Miami area. From downtown all the way up to Sunny Isles.

And underneath the artwork was the following tag line:

The Enchantment Group.
Magically transforming Miami in the blink of an eye.

"I'm sorry, sir," said Reginald. "But Miss Madalina has not yet returned."

Apparently, Madalina had gone out for a "girl's night" with Trish.

Woody stood, lost in space, in the grand foyer of La Connerie. "But it's after midnight."

"Twelve-fifty-four to be exact, sir. South Beach is, I'm afraid, a very late town. Can I fetch you a snack? Or perhaps a hot toddy?"

"No thanks. I think Sweetie and I are gonna crash."

"Without injury, I should dearly hope, sir."

"Me, too, Reg. Me, too."

★ ★ ★

"Voody!" sang Madalina in a mezzo-soprano-like voice. "I'm home!"

Even from across the room, Woody could smell the alcohol on her breath.

She tiptoed over to the bed and was about to lean over to kiss him when Sweetie growled and bared her teeth.

Shrieking, Madalina jumped back.

"Are you okay?"

"I do not think she like me no more."

"Sure, she does. Don't you, girl?"

Sweetie padded over to the far corner of the king-sized bed, turned her back to her master and slumped into a heap of self-pity.

"What a drama queen," he said, turning the light on next to his bed. "What time is it?"

"Four-thirty," she said, giggling. As if this was a perfectly normal hour to get home.

"You must have had a lot of fun."

"Oh, my God, you can't believe!"

Madalina rattled off a blow-by-blow description of her evening with her new best friend, Trish.

Dinner at Casa Tua—made even more fabulous when Jamie Foxx put their meals on his tab.

"Too many Buds" at Skybar.

A quick stopover at Mynt for vodka.

Followed by after-hours dancing at Mansion, an "absolute must for any clubgoer."

"Enough of me," she said. "I need to know! You have seen Prince?"

"Who?"

"Prince."

"Oh, what about him?"

Madalina slapped her hands to her hips and jutted out her chin. "Voody, do not make mess with me!"

"Who's messing with you?"

He was purposely drawing out the suspense to let her squirm.

"The Prince . . . well. . . ."

"What? What?"

"The Prince has agreed to take care of everything."

Madalina squealed and began to dance around the room. "Is fantastic!"

"All the necessary documents are contained in that briefcase over there on the dresser."

Woody reached over and presented Madalina with the tiny box he'd placed on the night table.

"As well as one other very important item."

Chapter 30

And so it came to pass that Woody awoke the following morning with a beautiful, naked Romanian ex-waitress curled up in his arms.

Within two seconds of accepting his proposal, Madalina had discarded her black Dolce & Gabbana minidress and La Perla undergarments and basically dragged Woody off the bed onto a bear-skin rug where she proceeded to raise his sails not once, but three times!

Anyway, they'd just fallen into a deep sleep when, a mere twenty-seven minutes later, Woody and his new fiancée were awakened by a loud rap on the door.

"Sorry to bother you, sir . . ."

The voice belonged to Reginald.

"But will you be needing the Phantom this morning?"

Woody's jaw muscles, stiff from all the extracurricular activity in which he had engaged, took a moment to loosen up.

"My what?"

"The Rolls, sir. To drive you to the office, of course."

Chapter 31

"What the hell do you mean the Tinnie land deal fell through?" bellowed Stanford Hollings with such force Todd feared his father's glass desk as well as each of the floor-to-ceiling windows of his corner office would shatter.

"The guy just got a better offer, Dad."

Todd waited to be castigated and condemned as though he'd machine-gunned a busload of schoolkids. He got a temporary stay of execution, however, when his father's assistant buzzed him.

"I thought I said no calls, Pamela . . . An emergency? . . . She wouldn't say? Damn it! Yes, put my wife through."

Todd leaned forward in his chair. "Is Mom all right?"

"Guess I'll find out right now, won't I?" said Stanford as he finger slapped the speakerphone button.

The gut-wrenching wails of Mrs. Hollings soon filled the room which, considering its square footage, was quite impressive.

"Ashley, Ashley! Get a hold of yourself for Christ's sake! What's wrong?"

Stanford was not the most comforting of husbands. Nor, for that matter, was he big on empathy with his kids.

"My, my party!"

Apparently, Ashley had planned to host a huge amfAR benefit at their house that evening. The cause didn't really matter to her. It was all about the A-list guests she'd invited.

"The, the chairwoman just called me. They've decided to change venues."

"The same day of the party?"

"Someone else offered to pay double their money! And promised to compensate us for canceling the caterers and everything else and—"

Ashley broke into hysterics again.

"Then it's a win-win situation as far as I'm concerned. Case closed. Take yourself a Valium, I've got real fires to put out here at the office."

And with that, Stanford Hollings abruptly terminated the call.

"Mom sounded really upset," said Todd.

"She'll go shopping and drown her sorrows. Anyway, not my concern. Right now I need to find out who the hell convinced Tinnie to sell his property!"

"Well, actually a company called The Enchantment Group brokered the deal."

"Never heard of them."

"Neither had I until today. But they've apparently got property all over South Florida. And beyond. In fact, you know that building going up across the street—"

"Of course," snapped his father. "Did you notice my head stuck up my ass? Place belongs to Trump."

"Not anymore it doesn't."

Stanford swiveled his chair around to witness for himself the forty-five-story tower which sure enough, according to the signage, had come under new ownership.

"I need the scoop on this company now!"

"We can Google it. Actually, that was what I was in the process of doing when you called me out of my office."

"Then what are you waiting for? DO IT NOW!"

Todd leapt from his seat. "You want me to use your computer?"

"Do I have to answer that question?" screamed his father, who only used the Internet to send e-mails.

Todd punched in the key words.

A blank blue screen popped up.

Followed by a soundtrack.

"Do you believe in magic?" said Stanford, who'd recognized that classic Lovin' Spoonful song from his junior high school days.

No sooner were those words spoken than they were treated to a slide show of the The Enchantment Group's many properties—those completed and those under construction—from West Palm Beach down to Coconut Grove; up the eastern seaboard to New York City; and across the continent to Los Angeles. With additional holdings in Chicago and Las Vegas.

"This is un-fucking-believable."

"Happened virtually overnight. I'm telling you, Dad, nobody saw this coming."

"But who is this guy? Where did he come from?"

Todd nearly shit in his pants when a photograph of The Enchantment Group's founder and CEO, Clarence Woods, came into focus.

Chapter 32

As much as he wanted to stay under the covers, Madalina insisted playing hooky was not an option. However, as Woody was now president of his own firm, it was permissible to delay his departure for a few more hours to attend to some more immediate business.

By the time Woody stumbled out of bed, he was on such a stoner high, nothing fazed him.

He cracked up when he saw his reflection in the mirror; dressed up like a corporate geek in that blue suit, white shirt and red tie.

He chortled when he saw the sumo-sized chauffeur standing by an arctic white Rolls Royce Phantom parked in the driveway.

He giggled in the backseat of the limo all the way from Star Island to One Eleven Brickell Avenue.

He peered, openmouthed, at the black glass monolith.

"This is my office building, I suppose."

Upon hearing confirmation, he doubled over in laughter.

In fact, by the time Woody traveled to the fortieth floor and entered the headquarters of The Enchantment Group, he was so hysterical, tears rolled down his cheeks, and his stomach muscles ached as if he'd done a million crunches.

"Good afternoon, Mr. Woods," said a polished woman behind a granite, tomb-sized console. "It's nice to see you so cheery."

"Believe me, you have no idea," he said, wiping his eyes. He
tried to keep a straight face. "I don't suppose you could please
point me in the direction of my, my, well, you know. My office?"

"Now that's pretty funny," said the receptionist joining him
in laughter.

"Uh-oh," she said in between snorts. "Talk about a mood
breaker. Here comes High Strung Howard."

A man charged up to Woody, his bald head shiny with perspiration, and his hooked nose even more out of joint. The position he held in the company was, of course, an unknown.

"Mr. Woods!" the guy gasped. "I've been trying to contact
you on your mobile all morning."

Woody was about to reach into his pants pocket when he
remembered he'd left the phone on the night table. Worse yet,
he'd shut the damn thing off when he and Madalina had tried to
catch a little shut-eye.

"Sorry about that. Is something, ah, wrong?"

"Just that we were expected at a ground-breaking ceremony
twenty-eight minutes ago. It's imperative we leave for Virginia
Key immediately."

Chapter 33

Virginia Key, like its neighbor Key Biscayne, was nestled between the bay and the Atlantic. But unlike the former, this island lacked a residential area. During the day, however, it was quite busy. Tourists flocked to the Miami Seaquarium, and scientists and students converged either at The Atlantic Oceanographic and Meteorological Lab, the Rosenstiel School of Marine and Atmospheric Science or the MAST Academy.

Virginia Key was also home to Jimbo's Shrimp Shack where, sitting by its picturesque lagoon (often used for photo shoots), one could play bocce ball, drink one-dollar beers and eat some of the "best damned smoked fish in the world." Provided you could find the place! The secret was to stay sharp and watch for an unmarked, unpaved street right past the MAST Academy known, in some guidebooks, as "Sewerline" because of a large waste-processing plant located on it. Take a sharp left and head straight. About a half mile in there is a fork in the road. Bear left and the seductive tang of Jimbo's smokehouse would guide you the rest of the way.

A right turn on this road, however, brings one to a subtropical coastal hammock and farther on to a pristine ocean beach with some of the most spectacular views of the city of Miami.

The owner of this rare ecological gem was one Gustavo

Tinnie, whose African-American grandmother, Eugenia Pickney, had become pregnant by her white boss, Archibald Tinnie, a wealthy Coconut Grove resident. Tinnie's barren wife, Eleanor, agreed to a divorce because, as the story went she, too, had taken a secret lover. A woman. Anyway, interracial taboos being what they were in the late 1800s, the couple fled by boat to Virginia Key where Archibald owned a four-hundred-plus-acre plot which funnily enough, he'd won in a drunken poker game. Basically as a consolation prize.

Fast forward to the twenty-first century. The original Tinnie homestead was destroyed in The Big Blow of 1926 and never rebuilt. And the last remaining member of the Tinnie clan, Gustavo, a life-long bachelor, had always been dead set against selling his ancestors' safe haven. But as taxes continued to rise, Gustavo had gotten squeezed into a financial predicament his salary as the owner of a jazz record label could not support.

Needless to say, when word of a potential sale of the property had been leaked to the press, local conservation groups had begun to prepare for the battle ahead.

When Woody was young, Katherine used to tell him stories about the ghosts of Eugenia and Archibald Tinnie whose paranormal mission was to keep any and all evil money-hungry developers at bay. She explained how the Tinnie property was a Mecca for indigenous plants and wildlife, many of which were listed as endangered by the State of Florida, and how the adjoining beach was a favorite place for sea turtles to lay their eggs in the sand. Nobody, save Mother Nature herself, was supposed to ever lay a finger on this land.

So it came as no surprise that once Woody realized where the Rolls was headed, he felt as if his head would explode.

"Shit," he groaned. "Shit. Shit, shit!"

"Are you all right?" asked High-Strung Howard.

"No, I am fucking horrible. Please tell me this is all a huge mistake."

Howard chuckled, as if his boss had cracked a joke. "Hardly, sir. This acquisition will no doubt be referred to as the real estate coup of the year. If not the decade!"

Woody peeked through the fingers covering his face and there, amidst a backdrop of red, black and white mangroves, he saw posted a tastefully designed recipe for disaster:

FUTURE SITE OF THE ENCHANTMENT TOWERS AND RESORT.

As sickening as those words were to read, this response paled in comparison to what Woody felt when he saw the fifty or so placard-toting men and women—the average age of whom was well over sixty-five—gathered on the beach along with a dozen or so of Miami's finest. Riot gear and all.

"This is bad. This is very bad," muttered Woody, rubbing his belly and swallowing bile.

"Oh, not to worry about them," said Howard. "We've dealt with those Sierra Club nuisances plenty of times. Hell, if it were up to them, we'd all be barefoot and living in tents with no running water." Howard placed a hand on Woody's shoulder. "Relax, Mr. Woods. It'll be fine."

Howard instructed the driver to park the Rolls alongside some saw palmetto trees and wild lantana bushes. He climbed out of the car first, but Woody stayed behind. Hanging on to his seat belt as if he were suspended from a piece of dental floss over the Grand Canyon.

"Mr. Woods, pardon me, but we really shouldn't keep our distinguished guests waiting any longer."

"Distinguished guests?"

"Why the Mayor of Miami, of course . . ."

As in Miguel Juan Carlos Diaz, GQ cover party boy. Hizzoner had been recently photographed (love those camera phones!) in the men's room of a South Beach club blowing a drag queen.

"And then there's Salvatore Pelligrino," said Howard, continuing. "From Magnum Construction. Carmela Feinstein from the Chamber of Commerce. Some members of the press. And of course, our guest of the hour—Mr. Gustavo Tinnie. Without him, this project would never have been."

Woody groaned again.

"I'm definitely going to be sick."

"Was it something you ate?"

"No, a fish I caught," he mumbled.

"Pardon?"

"Trust me, you don't wanna know."

Woody reluctantly emerged from his sanctuary into the warm, moist air of the hammock where he was greeted not by the sweet songs of pine siskins or Tennessee warblers, but by shrill chords of dissension.

"SAVE OUR NATURAL HABITATS!"

"DUMP DEVELOPMENT!"

"TINNIE, DON'T BE A SELLOUT!"

"ENCHANT THIS ASS!"

With Woody now sweating profusely, his clothes clung to his body like wilted lettuce. He couldn't have been more nauseous if he'd been locked inside a ship's hold with a ton of rotting squid. The end result being Woody lost it and spewed right on High-Strung Howard's shiny wingtips.

Profusely apologetic, Woody was about to clean off Howard's shoes when none other than his very own Aunt Katherine charged up to him. She was dressed for the occasion in battle fatigues: camouflage shorts, safari jacket and an Australian bush hat.

"Could have sworn it was you getting out of this car," she said. "But I had to come see for myself. What on earth are you doing here, Woody?"

"I was actually just about to ask myself that very question," said Woody.

He smiled sheepishly at Katherine and wiped off his mouth with the sleeve of his eighteen-hundred-dollar jacket.

"Something tells me you're not here to mess up those fancy-pants duds of yours, sugar."

Before he could address that issue, Howard, whose shoelaces were still peppered with vomit residue, butted into the conversation.

"Mr. Woods, excuse me for interrupting, but we really and truly need to move along here. Mayor Diaz wants to say a few words first, and then I've prepared you a short speech about how great an opportunity this is, yadda-yadda. There'll be a photo op, and finally you and Mr. Tinnie will do the honors of breaking ground."

Katherine looked at him with utter horror. "I understand my hearing has gone to shit, but I could swear that four-eyed pipsqueak said something that has the potential to cause me incredible distress. Woody, please tell me you are not playing a part in this travesty?"

Howard, clearly miffed by this affront to his physicality, took it upon himself to answer the question for his boss.

"Mr. Woods happens to be the CEO and President of The Enchantment Group. And, as of today, Mr. Woods is the owner of this property which, for your information, whoever you are, he plans to transform into a five-star luxury development the likes of which Miami has never seen before."

Katherine was dumbfounded. An event as rare as say, the Pope riding bare-ass on a Harley in the Macy's Thanksgiving Day Parade.

"I know you're going to find this hard to believe," said Woody. "But the truth is I'm just as surprised as you are."

"How the hell could you not know!" screamed Katherine. "Don't you lie to me, Clarence!"

As if things had not gotten complicated enough, Dorothy and

her granddaughter, Kristin—clad in grubby shorts, a Greenpeace T-shirt and a red bandana—suddenly appeared.

"What the hell are you doing here?" Dorothy asked.

"Wait until you hear this one," said Katherine, filling her friends in on the details.

Kristin turned to Woody. "The Enchantment Group? That's impossible. Was your body taken over by a blood-thirsty, money-grubbing alien or something?"

"I'm telling you," said Woody. "I had no clue this land was part of the bargain."

The mouths of Dorothy and Kristin dropped open.

"But how could you possibly come into all this overnight?" asked Kristin.

"If I told you, you'd never believe me," said Woody.

"You're not running drugs, are you?" asked Dorothy.

"Don't be ridiculous. Not everybody in Miami is involved in drugs."

"That loaded older woman," said Katherine. "She behind this?"

"What older woman?"

Woody had clearly forgotten about the alibi he had invented the other night.

"Look," said Katherine. "At this point I don't give a rat's ass who owns this deed or who paid for it. Or who has the money or who doesn't. I just don't want anyone to touch this land. Period."

Howard glared at her. "What you have suggested is not only unreasonable but a complete impossibility."

"I don't see why we can't leave the property as is," said Woody. "Turn it into a, you know, nature preserve. Hiking trails. That sort of thing."

"I'm afraid this is absolutely impossible," said Howard.

Not only had all the dotted lines been signed, but construction was slated to start the following day. Hundreds of jobs were on the line. Not to mention the stellar reputation of The Enchantment Group.

"If we pulled out of this deal," said Woody's right-hand man, "the company would become the laughingstock of the industry, and we'd be sued into financial oblivion."

"Shit, shit, shit," said Woody, feeling as if he was going to barf again.

"Clarence, I'm warning you. Fix this mess or things are going to get mighty ugly around here."

Howard fluffed up his chest, flared his nostrils and got right in Katherine's face.

"Excuse me, but do you have a permit to gather such as you have?"

"Actually, no," said Katherine. "This powwow was a rather last minute thing."

"In that case, I need you and your friends on the beach to pull up stakes and go home."

"Oh, come on!" exclaimed Kristin. "Nobody is being disruptive."

"Nobody is being disruptive—YET," snapped Katherine.

"Well then, I'm afraid no permit, no protest."

And with that, Howard called to one of the cops for assistance.

"I'm going to ask you all one more time. Nicely. Please disband your group and leave now."

"Like hell we will! In fact, you can all kiss my sweet New Orleans ass!"

"But, Aunt Katherine . . ."

"Don't you Aunt Katherine me, boy! If you don't fix this mess you've dug yourself into, you are no longer my nephew!"

★ ★ ★

Before the day was out, the future home of The Enchant-ment Towers and Resort became a seething sinkhole from hell.

First, the gold-plated shovels with which the ground was supposed to be ceremoniously broken went missing. Next, Gustavo Tinnie was "abducted." He'd wandered off for a pee and had just pulled up the zipper of his bright blue linen pants when Dorothy's granddaughter, Kristin, along with Joe Slavanik, a three-hundred-pound former NFL linebacker from the late '60s, snuck up behind him. Unfortunately, Gustavo, already fear-ful his dead ancestors might make an unscheduled appearance, was so taken by surprise, he fainted dead-away.

Tinnie was rushed off to Mercy Hospital. Kristin, and her partner in crime, Joe Slavanik, were arrested and charged with attempted kidnapping. This act of "social injustice" naturally did not sit well with the remaining demonstrators.

High-Strung Howard managed to trip over one of his shoe-laces and twisted his ankle so badly it was almost a compound fracture. Woody instructed his driver, Ernie, to transport Howard to Mercy Hospital and then drive him home.

Mayor Diaz, who was late for his haircut and pedicure ap-pointment, tried to sneak off. Only to discover one of the tires of his new Land Cruiser had been slashed and the words "male whore" had been written in red lipstick on his windshield.

"Book the whole fucking lot of them!" exclaimed the mayor, whose patience had long ago been lost.

Meanwhile, the paddy wagons, which had been delayed by an overturned truck hauling chickens on I–95, finally arrived. A good many of the demonstrators refused to go peacefully. Some actually taunted the cops with their walkers or canes. Others— Katherine and Dorothy included—lay down on the ground and had to be carried off. But no matter how diverse the choices of civil disobedience, these senior citizens were united by their pledge to "fight against environmental injustices."

Needless to say, the press had quite a field day.

Woody had no power to rescind the charges of disorderly conduct, trespassing and resisting arrest, but he could offer to post bail for everybody. This proposal was refused. Nobody wanted anything to do with what Katherine described as her "former nephew's double-crossing, self-serving, conniving generosity." Period.

And as his aunt was carried into the paddy wagon, she pointed a finger at Woody.

"Who on earth are you?" she yelled.

"I'm not quite sure I know," he replied. "But up until this afternoon, I thought I was the luckiest guy on the planet."

Chapter 34

By the time the limo crossed over the bridge to Star Island, Woody had reached a decision.

The fantasy had to end.

He'd spend a nice quiet evening with Madalina and, after a beer or two, work up the courage to break the news.

"Whoa, what's up with all this traffic, Ernie?"

The chauffeur shook his head. "Looks like maybe chou having lots of peeples for deener, Meester Woods."

Determined to investigate, Ernie swerved over to the left and drove up to the front of the line. Two portly men dressed in black and armed with clipboards and headsets guarded the entrance to La Connerie.

"Let us through, man," said Ernie.

The shorter of the two men pointed to Woody. "Is he on the list?"

After the hellish day he'd had, Woody had no patience for this shit. He rolled down his window. "Look, I kind of live here, so could you please let me through?"

"If you kinda live here, then how come you don't know about this party here tonight?"

"Ah, look, man. I've had a lot of unexplainable, irrational

things happen to me in the past week, so nothing fazes me any-more."

"Maybe this is a surprise party. It your birthday or some-thing?"

"No, not for eight months, actually."

"Diego," piped in the other guard. "I told you before; this here is a charity benefit. You need to pay a lot of money to get in."

"How much?" asked Woody.

"Twenty-five clams."

"Twenty-five dollars? That's not so bad."

"No, two thousand five hundred bucks!"

"What are chou loco?" yelled Ernie, whose Latin temper had begun to sizzle. "Dis ees Meester Woods! Chou let heem in right now!"

"I'm sorry," said Diego. "But I still must see some identifica-tion."

"As you wish," said Woody. He fished out his wallet and handed over his license.

"The address ain't the same."

Ernie, who was the width and height of both men com-bined, stormed out of the car and got right into Diego's face. Whatever he told the guy apparently worked because within a nanosecond, the Rolls was waved through.

"Lemme get the door for you, Meester Woods."

Woody gathered the jacket and puke-stained tie crumpled up on the seat. "It's okay, Ernie. I got it. Thanks for your help."

"Is my pleasure, Meester Woods. See you tomorrow morn-ing."

Not if I have anything to do with it, thought Woody.

Meanwhile, in comparison with the formally attired men and women stepping from their luxury vehicles, Woody must have looked like a train wreck in a field of lilacs. Not that he gave a shit. His slacks were dirty. His shirt wrinkled and unbuttoned. Sleeves rolled unfashionably high up his shoulders. His face, shellacked with dried sweat, and his new coiffure, a wreck.

Reginald ran out to greet him.

"Here you are, sir. We've been anxiously awaiting your arrival."

"Sorry, but I've been through hell and back."

"You certainly look the part, sir. Miss Madalina has been very worried about you. Especially because she couldn't reach you all day."

"I forgot to bring my cell phone. Where is she, by the way?"

"Out back with all the guests. I suppose you'd like to, ah, freshen up a bit prior to joining her," he said.

Woody took an indelicate whiff of his armpit and grimaced. "That sounds like it might be a good idea."

"If you don't mind, sir, I'm going to reserve comment."

Woody followed the butler up the stairs. "I must say I wasn't exactly expecting to come home to all this. What's going on?"

"It's a fund-raiser for amfAR, sir. If you're not familiar with this organization, it is one of the world's leading nonprofits dedicated to the support of HIV/AIDS research, HIV prevention, treatment education and advocacy of sound AIDS-related public policy."

The last time Woody wore a tuxedo, it was to his senior prom. He and his best friend, Eric—now a celebrity chef at a top New York restaurant—had decided it would be a goof (in an iconoclastic way) to escort each other rather than face possible rejection from some girl. Anyway, Woody had found the rented tuxedo so uncomfortable he had to "self-medicate" with weed and beer in order to get through the evening.

"There you go, sir," said Reginald, who graciously agreed to help Woody fasten that stupid cummerbund and tie his bow tie.

"I feel like a damn penguin," he said, fidgeting in front of the mirror.

"An exceptionally well-dressed penguin, indeed, sir. You look smashing."

Needless to say, Woody was not convinced.

"Ms. Madalina requested that you wear this tonight."

Reginald handed him a rectangular box which contained a rose gold chronograph Bvlgari along with a note:

To my handsome king.

I ♥ You.

Madalina.

Put this way, Woody had no choice but to remove his father's old Swiss Army watch and replace it with her gift. At least, until the end of the evening.

Woody turned to Sweetie. After having perched herself on the bed, the dog had been watching her master's every move with much interest.

"So what do you think about this getup?"

She merely yawned and cocked her head as if to say, *Trust me, you don't wanna know.*

"Hmm, that good, huh? I'm so not ready for this tonight," he groaned.

"May I suggest a glass of Cristal to perhaps smooth out the creases?" asked Reginald.

"No champagne, thanks. But if it's possible, I could really go for a cold brew."

On the back lawn, between the house and the edge of the bay, an enormous, open-sided Moroccan tent now stood. The ceiling was draped with billowing layers of white gauze from which hung hundreds of cherry-sized blue lights. One end of the tent was covered with oriental carpeting upon which sat low-lying beds strewn with a multitude of colored pillows. Very

Arabian Nights decadent. The other end was reserved for more formal dining. Elaborately set tables with exotic flower arrangements and antique brass Mogador lanterns. A parquet dance floor was positioned in the middle of the tent along with a raised stage for a live band.

Bud in hand, Woody stood on the veranda. He hadn't yet mustered up the courage to join the party and chose to watch the scene from afar. The visuals were rather boring but the music was great. A quartet was playing "*Soon all will know*," a tune he recognized from one of his favorite Wynton Marsalis CD's. Damn, if the trumpeter didn't both sound and look like Marsalis himself.

"Hey, Woody!"

It was Fred Sage. Decked out in a black-on-black tuxedo with a white, fringed scarf draped around his shoulders. He was, of course, accompanied by his fiancée, Trish, whose body was covered in strategically placed clusters of silver sequins.

"Is that actually you?"

"Afraid so," said Woody.

"You look so handsome," said Trish, who despite the formality of the evening was blowing bubbles with her gum.

"Thanks, but I feel like an asshole dressed in these clothes."

"You know what I say," said Fred. "It's fine to look like an asshole as long as you don't smell like one."

Trish hit Fred with her evening bag. "That was like totally disgusting!" She turned to Woody. "That man has no class."

Fred shrugged his shoulders. "Who needs class when you've got all this cash? Speaking of which, I saw the ring on Madalina's finger. That musta set you back plenty."

"You have no idea," said Woody.

As in selling his soul to the devil.

"Are you going to just stand there like a wallflower all night?" asked Fred.

"Actually, I do need to hook up with Madalina."

"We can go with you," said Trish.

Woody begged off. "Nah, you guys go ahead. I'm going to stay here and finish my beer first."

"Oh, my God," squealed Trish. "There's Enrique Iglesias and his girlfriend, that tennis player—what's her name? Maybe I can get an autograph . . ."

And with that, she dragged Fred off toward the action.

Woody waited another ten minutes or so and then slowly walked along the torch-lit path to the tent. By his estimation, there must have been about four hundred guests. A competitive interplay of diamonds, couture, attitudes and the handiwork of some of the best plastic surgeons du jour. Outside of a few random smiles from some women (mostly older and probably single), he found himself adrift in a sea of strangers he had no intention of ever getting to know.

Woody picked up a program from one of the tables and scanned it. As far as entertainment, well, his eyes and ears hadn't deceived him. That guy playing the trumpet was none other than the master himself. Along with Allen Toussaint on the piano, Nathan East on base and Steve Gadd on drums. Woody was less impressed, however, to learn that the evening's "star" performer was Beyoncé, who was scheduled to sing "four songs off her latest album." Sure, Woody had heard of her, but never in this lifetime would he be caught dead listening to that so-called music.

He was standing there, basically lost in space, when someone grabbed him from behind and covered his eyes.

"Guess who?"

The accent immediately revealed the person's identity, but he played dumb. "Gee, I haven't a clue."

But when Woody turned around, he almost didn't recognize Madalina. She wore a red strapless gown which punctuated every one of her curves with an exclamation point, and her hair was upswept with a diamond tiara.

"Whoa," was all he could say. "Whoa."

"You like?"

Although he still preferred her in a T-shirt and shorts or better yet naked, she was quite a vision.

"You're beyond beautiful."

"And you, Voody. You are so handsome in tuxedo I pick for you." She examined his wrist. "You wear watch, yes. Do you like?"

"Yes," he said, telling a white lie. "It was a really thoughtful gift, but Madalina, we really need to have a talk about all this later. In the meantime, I'd love to whisk you off to a dark corner and—"

"Not now. Later. I promise I will make up to you big-time, yes? You know thing I do with my tongue . . ."

The mere image of that little trick of hers gave him the shudders.

"But now I must introduce you to someone very special."

"By the way," said Woody as he followed her through the crowd. "I'm really curious. How on earth did you put together this party so quickly?"

She smiled. "Easy. I use your American Express black credit card. You pick up phone to speak to concierge and anything is possible."

"Mr. and Mrs. Trump, I would like you to meet my fiancé, Clarence."

Claire-rance?

"Very nice to meet you," he said, shaking their hands. "But seriously, please call me Woody."

"Well, Woody," said Mr. Trump. "It's a pleasure to meet you as well. Congratulations on Virginia Key. Although I have to confess, I'm a bit envious old man Tinnie took your offer and not mine."

This remark caused the beer sitting in Woody's stomach to ferment into toxic waste. He feared the worst, but then again, he entertained the personal satisfaction he'd earn by hurling over The Donald's shoes.

Madalina picked up the void left by Woody's inability to respond. "Like you have said, Mr. Trump, and I make quote of you. 'The thrill of the deal is all about winning.' Yes?"

The Donald grinned at her. "Looks like I certainly won't be seeing you in the board room tonight, my dear."

Never having watched *The Apprentice* on television, Woody failed to find the humor in this remark.

But alas, what was about to transpire next would be far from a laughing matter.

Chapter 35

Woody watched the three people elbow their way through the crowd. Although dressed for the occasion, they were clearly not in the mood to party.

"Look who showed up," he whispered to Madalina. "Did you actually invite them?"

Before she had a chance to answer, Ashley Hollings—dressed in a silver Carolina Herrera off-the-shoulder gown—stormed up to Madalina.

"You little cunt!"

Ashley projected her voice with such power she gained the attention of eighty-nine-point-six percent of the revelers.

Sensing a media-juicy story, a rookie reporter from the local TV show "Deco Drive" put her cameraman on red alert.

"Who the hell do you think you are to steal this event, my event that I've been working on for three fucking months, right from under me?"

"I did not steal," said Madalina. Her self-composure was impressive. "I just make better offer."

"Offer my ass, you social-climbing two-timer! Made me look like a complete fool. Mark my words, missy. This is your last stand. I'll ruin you in this town! Ruin you!"

Ashley Hollings took a deep yoga breath and grinned triumphantly at the crowd.

Her husband, Stanford, stepped forward.

"Perhaps you all are not cognizant of the fact," he said in an equally thunderous voice. "That our host tonight is about to come under criminal investigation."

Gasps ricocheted from one person to another.

"I've done nothing outside the law," said Woody.

"Oh, really? This supposed company of yours, this Enchantment Group. It just materialized out of thin air, and now you own some of the hottest properties in town and across the country. How is this possible, please tell me?"

"Maybe I just have an aptitude for the business," said Woody.

"Bullshit," said Todd, who decided to enter the conversation. "Nobody goes from working as a dock boy one day to a real estate mogul the next."

"Hey, man, it's America. This is the ultimate rags-to-riches story."

The crowd snickered amongst themselves which only pissed off young Hollings.

"If you find that amusing, listen up. The last time I saw her," he said, pointing to Madalina, "she was waiting tables. And doing a shitty job at that. Not so in the bedroom, though. I gotta say she is one Euro whore who knows how to take international relations to a new level."

"Did you sleep with that asshole?"

"NO! Todd—*Toad*—he makes big shit lie!"

"The hell I do, babe. You couldn't wait to get into my pants and my bank account."

Madalina lunged for Todd and kneed him right between the balls. Whereupon Ashley came to the rescue of her baby boy.

And just like that, the "party of the season" was on its way to being declared a disaster area before the cocktail hour was over.

Chapter 36

About five minutes after security escorted a certain family from the premises, their replacements arrived. In droves.

Feline-sized vermin, to be exact. None of whom had paid the ticket price, but still intended to be well fed.

The guests, however, had no intention of socializing with this subelement of society. A stampede ensued.

Tables were overturned. Glasses broken. Plates smashed. Birds-of-paradise and orchids strewn over the floor and trampled like cheap carnations. A severed stiletto heel here. Someone's toupee there. Tributaries of alcohol flowed throughout the entire tent.

The rats were not picky and demolished every hors d'oeuvre available. Foie gras from Fauchon in Paris. Beluga caviar on buckwheat blinis. Wagyu Kobe beef capriccio. Hamachi tartar with gold leaf. To name a few delicacies.

And then as quickly as they arrived, the creatures scattered off to crash another party on the island. Perhaps at Rosie O'Donnell's estate if Donald Trump had anything to do with choice of location.

Needless to say, Beyoncé's performance was cancelled.

Woody was convinced this egregious prank had been engineered and paid for (no doubt, for a hefty price) by none other than the Hollings clan.

Madalina had plunked herself down on the empty dance floor. Her gown torn and stained. Her tiara hanging off the side of her head. Weeping and chugging a bottle of Stoli. But despite puffy bloodshot eyes and smeared cosmetics, Woody still found her incredibly beautiful. He wrapped an arm around her freckled bare shoulder and brought her close to him. Madalina mumbled something he couldn't translate and then buried her face in his chest.

Although the rancid taste of Todd's accusation still lingered, this was certainly not the time to bring up that subject. Besides, it was he, not that prick, who had won Madalina's heart. And that's all that mattered now.

"Did I ever tell you how much I love the way you smell?"

"I am wearing new perfume," she said, sniffing. "Is called Heiress. By Paris Hilton. I invite her to party but she never come."

"Guess for her sake, she's lucky she didn't," he said, chuckling.

Madalina clearly didn't appreciate the joke.

"Look, we had our fun, sampled the so-called good life, which in my opinion ain't all its cracked up to be, but don't you think it's time for us to return to the real world? This house. The real estate. The clothes. The money. The cars. It's all bullshit."

"What do you say to me, Voody?"

"I want Raymond, the fish, to take back everything he gave to me. I want my old life back. When things were simple. Uncomplicated. I mean, that is how we should be together."

"But we have nothing then."

Woody swallowed hard before he spoke. "We'll have each other."

She stared hard at him for a moment and then, cackling like a Harpy, pushed him away.

"Are you stupid, crazy boy? You want me to go back to shit? After I have given you my body! My heart! After I trust for you to care for me."

"I'll always take care of you, Madalina. You and me, we can do this together. We don't need that much. Besides, aren't m-m-married people who love each other supposed to accept each other in, you know, sickness and in health and for richer or poorer and . . ."

"You want for me to have shit life like I have in Romania?"

"But it won't be like that, Madalina. I mean, maybe we can get our old jobs back at the club."

"And where will we live?"

"Once I get back on my aunt Katherine's good side, we can stay at the house on Key Biscayne. She's quite a character, but you'll love her. And then in about eight months, after I finish my boat, we can set sail for what I can almost guarantee will be the trip of a lifetime. Think of the adventures we can have. Madalina, I want to be with you forever and I promise I'll do everything in my power to make you happy."

Gazing deeply into his eyes, Madalina raised his hand to her mouth and began to seductively suck on one of his fingers.

"You say you want to make me happy, yes?"

"Of, of, of course I do."

"Then we must make revenge on shit people who treat us with such disrespect."

She unraveled his bowtie, removed the black pearl studs from his shirt and slowly ran her tongue down his torso.

"But, but how, Madalina?"

"You must go back and speak to Prince one last time . . ."

Chapter 37

Woody's pulse quickened as he pulled into the driveway of West Mashta Drive. Although Katherine had booked herself an overnighter at the Miami–Dade lockup, he still fretted about running into her. Especially now that he had been "disowned."

All the lights were off. But then again, it was after midnight. Even if his aunt had been home, she never stayed up this late.

"Shh," Woody whispered to his dog. "No noise."

He removed his shoes, turned the key in the lock and ever so slowly opened the door. It squeaked miserably. Woody made a mental note to oil those metal hinges.

Next, Woody tiptoed into the kitchen and flicked on a small light over the stove. He was surprised to find Katherine had left her breakfast dishes in the sink. Evidence that she had split in a hurry for Virginia Key. The thought of which caused his stomach to react. Woody needed something to get rid of that godawful taste in his mouth, so he stole a handful of homemade pecan tassies from the cookie jar and downed nearly a quart of chocolate milk. Basically the only food he'd had since that morning.

Next he peeked in Katherine's room. No sign of her there either. The bed was untouched. It gave him some pleasure to see that "Mack," the two-foot-long plush stuffed shark he'd given her as a birthday gift years ago, had not been tossed. His eyes shifted over to her night table on which sat three framed photos: Herb, before he went bald, a wedding portrait, and one of himself, aged ten, proudly standing in front of the fourteen-foot skiff he and Herb had built. As well as some grisly serial killer mystery (strange how she loved those stupid books), an aromatherapy candle and her blood pressure medication.

He felt even more like a complete shit and closed her door behind him.

Woody next headed for his room and grabbed his banjo.

"All right," he said to Sweetie. "Time to take care of business."

The dog responded with an affirmative *woof* and followed her master. However, she flat-out declined an invitation to accompany him outside.

Knowing his pooch as well as he did, this uncustomary behavior could mean only one thing.

A storm was imminent.

All the signs were there.

The air was heavy with moisture and stank of rotting fish and sulfur.

The wind—judging from those ubiquitous long-crested waves out in the bay—was gusting forty, fifty miles an hour.

The sky—dark and sepia-colored—hung with low horizontal arcus clouds, the undersides of which were boiling and turbulent.

Hell, even the ballsiest of sailors would opt to play landlubber on a night like this.

As the waves pummeled the seawall, Woody struggled to stay vertical. He didn't care if his stupid tux got wet, but he doubted the saltwater spray was the best thing for his banjo.

His fingers tightened around the instrument's neck. He wondered if the sound of his music would be heard above the roar of the pounding surf and howling winds.

No sooner had he completed one refrain of "Foggy Mountain

Breakdown," than Mother Nature responded with a round of deafening "applause" followed by an impressive light show.

"Raymond!" shouted Woody.

"Over here!"

He shined his flashlight in the direction of the voice, and sure enough, there was the fish struggling to keep his head above water.

"Well, look at you all dressed up! Talk about curb appeal! That a custom-made Oxxford tuxedo you got on?"

"I don't know and I don't care. No offense, Raymond, but I didn't come here to talk fashion . . ."

"WAIT!"

His heart fell into his shoes.

"Madalina!" he exclaimed, turning around. "You're not supposed to be here!"

"I do not trust you to tell Prince what I want, so I come to make sure you do."

Her hair was loose and she had changed into jeans, a tight white sweater and flip-flops. Although seductively appealing, Woody had to stay focused.

"I told you I would think about it, but the truth is I reached the same conclusion. I just can't do this anymore, Madalina."

She glowered at him, oozing venom. Woody half expected to turn to stone any minute.

"Who cares about you? You are nothing to me now! Nothing!"

And with that the girl stormed up to the seawall, steadied herself as best she could against the elements and yelled at the top of her lungs.

"You must make ME, Madalina Drajoi, richest person in all of world! You must make me as rich as Mr. Bill Gates!"

The heavens erupted with thunder of apocalyptic proportions, illuminating Biscayne Bay as brightly as the sunniest of all days.

"I hate to inform you, toots," said Raymond Prince, laughing. "But nobody, not even God, is as rich as Bill Gates."

"I do not care, you stupid, ugly creature. You must give me what I ask!"

"Sorry, but this contract has now been officially declared null and void!"

Before Woody had a chance to respond, Raymond Prince—his friend, his mentor, his nemesis—was gone.

And in his place came the deluge. With a vengeance.

"Come back!" screamed Madalina. "Come back! I demand. Come back!"

She stomped her feet on the ground, slipped and fell on her ass. Despite how horribly she'd treated him, Woody offered his assistance.

"Do not touch me!"

"But, Madalina . . ."

Shouting at him in Romanian, she stood up, ripped his banjo out of his hands, smashed it against the concrete seawall and ran off. Woody stared in disbelief at the wood-splintered remains of the instrument he had treasured for so many years.

The sound of an engine roused him from his stupor.

Sprinting to the front of the house, he arrived just as a Rolls Royce Phantom pulled out of the driveway and sped up the road.

Unsure which way to turn, the mastless hull of the *Sea Sponge* came into focus.

As always, still there for him.

Woody, feeling very much like a contrite lover, ascended the ladder and climbed into the cockpit. He aimed to seek shelter from the storm down below and opened the hatch. But unfortunately, as Woody was not wearing his rubber-soled shoes but a pair of velvet dress shoes, he lost his footing on the rain-slicked steps.

Smacking his head on the overhang.

Whereupon the poor boy was knocked stone cold.

Chapter 38

The next morning Woody awoke to a multitude of wet, tender kisses from an adoring female.

Namely his dog.

Woody started to slough off the saliva from his face when he felt a very tender knot in the upper left corner of his forehead. It was then that he realized he was not tucked under the bedcovers but sprawled on top of a wooden slab in the sleeping quarters of the very vessel that would some day transport him around the globe.

Wearing paint-stained shorts, an America's Cup T-shirt and his Teva flip-flops.

His Swiss Army watch firmly affixed to his wrist.

Given the ferocity of last night's storm, the backyard appeared completely untouched. Not one puddle. Not one fallen branch or palm tree frond. None of the patio furniture overturned.

Woody heard the TV blasting. This gave him pause considering his aunt was supposed to have slept elsewhere. He slid open the glass door, removed his shoes and cautiously tiptoed into the kitchen. Sweetie following in his footsteps.

There she was at the stove stirring a pot of her dreadful oatmeal.

"Aunt Katherine?"

"Oh my," she screamed, grasping her chest. "You gave me quite a fright! I may not even need any caffeine this morning."

"How did you get here? I thought you were in jail."

"Really? Don't exactly remember breaking the law."

Woody was really confused. "Are you still angry with me?"

"For what? You clog up the toilet again?"

"No, about what happened yesterday at Gustavo Tinnie's land."

She stared at him hard. "Have you recently lost your mind?"

Given the chain of recent events, Woody wasn't sure how to answer that question.

Katherine put down her spoon, walked up close to her nephew and gave him the once over. "Look at that nasty bump on your head."

"It's nothing."

Of course, his aunt refused to accept this diagnosis.

"Maybe you've got yourself a concussion. Could explain the strange behavior and . . ."

Needless to say, Woody didn't wait for Katherine to finish her sentence.

The Porsche was no longer parked in the driveway. In its place stood Woody's battered and dented Chevy, beautifully restored to its original rusted state.

He looked inside. The seats were once again covered in a thick layer of dog hair. That wad of gum was stuck on the carburator-stained carpet. His eclectic collection of junk strewn about. But perhaps most important, there, behind the front seat, was his father's banjo. With nary a scratch, nor a nick.

The really big question remained, however. Had the rest of the pieces of the puzzle been put back in their proper places?

In a flash, Woody was behind the wheel of his truck.

His first stop was Virginia Key. He made such a sharp turn onto Sewerline, a mushroom cloud of dust exploded behind him. He bore right at the fork, traveled several hundred yards but could go no further. There, stretched across the road, was a fence and a padlocked gate upon which hung a sign familiar to Woody as well as other curiosity seekers through the years:

Private property.

Keep out!

Trespassers will be prosecuted within the full extent of the law.

Woody found a towering black-glass office building at One Eleven Brickell Avenue. He double-parked the pickup out front and ran inside the building. He was immediately stopped by security.

"Are the headquarters for a real estate company named The Enchantment Group located in this building?"

Apparently not, as he was soon to learn.

Woody crossed the bridge and drove up to the gatehouse.

"Can I help you, sir?" asked the guard, giving him the once-over.

"Guess you don't recognize me, but I live at Number Six Star Island Drive. You know, La Connerie."

"Nice try buddy," he said with a sneer. "That place, which used to be called Wind Song, has been boarded up and empty for the past four years. And, by the way, Einstein, I take it you don't know what la connerie means?"

"Haven't a clue," said Woody.

"Well, I'm French Canadian, and translated, *la connerie* is actually slang for—how can I put this—bullshit!"

Woody's trek to The Summit in South Beach also proved to be a bust.

He didn't get past the guardhouse, let alone ascend the elevator to his former penthouse apartment!

And as for that little apartment back on Key Biscayne, well, according to the super, nobody other than Wanda Cooper and "her six fuckin' cats" had ever lived at 135 Sunrise Road.

Woody made it from Key Biscayne to Coconut Grove in twelve minutes flat and turned into the entrance to the Trade Winds Yacht Club.

Big Bill saluted him and opened up the gate.

So far, so good, thought Woody.

He parked his truck in the employees' lot and had just walked past the tennis courts when he ran into Skip Edwards and Ariel Vega.

"What the hell are you doing here?" barked his boss.

Uh-oh, thought Woody. Busted.

"Look, Skip, I'm really sorry and, and . . ."

"If you're apologizing for getting here late, don't worry about it, son. I tried to call you at the house before you left, but Katherine said I just missed you. Anyway, that gig you scheduled with Ted Sage . . ."

"You getting real soft in the head, boss." said Ariel. "It's Fred Sage."

"Oh shit!" exclaimed Woody. "I completely forgot about him."

"Not to worry, son. Asshole up and cancelled this morning. Sorry, I know you could have used the extra cash. Anyway, I just wanted to save you a damn trip in."

Ariel pointed to the bump on Woody's forehead. "What the hell did you do to yourself?"

"Long story. Not worth telling."

For the simple reason that no one would ever believe it anyway.

"In that case," said Skip. "Why are you standing here with your thumb up your ass? It's your day off, son. Go home! As for me, I really need to go take a piss."

Everything is as it was, thought Woody. Reality never felt so good.

"Oh, yeah," said Ariel. "I got some bad news for you. About that new waitress. You know, the one you were all hot over."

It was almost inconceivable that Woody had completely forgotten about Madalina. But the truth was, he had.

His chest tightened. "Is she all right?"

"She gone, man."

"What do you mean, gone?"

"She called Elizabeth last night and said she wasn't coming back to work at the club. Said someone made her an offer she just couldn't refuse."

Chapter 39

Woody poured a glass of chocolate milk and propped himself against the refrigerator.

"What's for dinner? I'm starving."

"Like this is a revelation," said Katherine. "We're having baked cheese grits, okra, grilled tuna and . . ."

Woody was so taken aback by the mere mention of a certain fish, he blew milk out of his nostrils.

"You all right, sugar?"

He dried his face with a paper towel. "Yeah, yeah, fine. Just a fly flew up my nose."

"Oh, by the way, I asked Dorothy and Kristin to join us for dinner."

Katherine folded her arms over her chest and eyeballed him. As if waiting to butt heads.

"Cool," came the unanticipated response.

"Did you say cool?"

"Yep, cool," he said, taking pleasure in totally disarming his aunt. "I'm going to take a shower."

Katherine cleared her throat and shuffled over to the oven with a casserole dish. "Sugar, my hands are full. Could you please put on the five o'clock news before you go?"

He switched the channel to her favorite local station and

was just about to head out of the kitchen when he heard a banjo playing a very familiar tune. "Foggy Mountain Breakdown" to be exact.

"So come on down and pay us a visit today . . ."

Woody stopped dead in his tracks.

"We'll give you a deal you won't forget. All you gotta do is ASK!"

The gender—male.

The accent—pure Brooklynese.

The intonation—nasal.

Woody turned and jumped in front of the television.

"I'm Raymond Prince. . . ."

The man was in his midforties, a bit pudgy with slicked-back salt-and-pepper hair, a cleft chin and a square jaw. He had an ermine cape thrown over his shoulders and a crown on his head. His arm was wrapped around a petite woman clad in a gold lamé gown. An ornate diamond and emerald tiara affixed her streaked blond locks.

"And this is my princess. My lovely wife, Sandy."

The television camera then panned across a lot filled with luxury cars.

"Come visit our kingdom," they said in unison. "Prince Motor City. Where all your dreams come true!"

Once Woody managed to unlock his chin from his chest, he burst into laughter.

"What on earth is so funny?" asked Katherine.

He wiped the tears from his eyes and shook his head.

"Just some silly inside joke which, trust me, is certainly not worth revisiting."

Epilogue

KATHERINE ARNOLD never won the Big Bang three-hundred-million-dollar jackpot. Her plans to purchase the Virginia Key property from GUSTAVO TINNIE had to be scrubbed, but her dream to have the land turned into a nature sanctuary was realized after she managed to convince Gustavo (specifically with a home-cooked Cajun meal and numerous Bloody Marys) to turn the land over to the State of Florida.

Meanwhile, Katherine and Gustavo discovered they had more in common than environmental issues, and are now, officially, an item.

DOROTHY LITTLE traded in her Cadillac for a hybrid Prius and found herself a "sixty-eight-year-old boy toy" at bingo.

TODD HOLLINGS and his best friend, BARRY FELDS, went hiking in Montana where, after getting lost in the hills for a week, they had a "Brokeback Mountain" moment. Incapable of "quitting" each other, they have since run off to Key West where they've opened up a very successful bed and breakfast. They also raise Yorkshire terriers.

SKIP EDWARDS retired happily to an island in the Bahamas where he purportedly swims naked every morning and takes great pleasure in pissing wherever and whenever he wants.

ELIZABETH VEGA left the Trade Winds Yacht Club and opened up a Jamaican/Cuban restaurant with her husband ARIEL in South Beach. Since Brad Pitt and Angelina Jolie sampled her cuisine, business is booming.

MADALINA DRAJOI married eighty-year-old GREGORY COX, formerly of the Trade Winds Geezer Patrol, in a quiet ceremony on the Isle of Capri. After Mr. Cox dropped dead on their wedding night, Madalina inherited five-point-five million dollars. Unfortunately, Mr. Cox's son contested the will and she got nothing. However, Madalina did manage to earn herself a spot on the television show *The Apprentice*. After beating a male graduate of Harvard Business School, she is currently working for Donald Trump and has just agreed to pose for *Playboy* for one million dollars.

FRED SAGE was arrested for tax fraud and is serving a two-year sentence at a white-collar penitentiary. His wine collection was auctioned off at Sotheby's in order to pay his legal fees, and he has since let his hair go gray. His fiancée, TRISH was booked on shoplifting charges after she got caught stuffing a Dolce and Gabbana dress into her Chanel bag. Her wedding to Fred has been permanently postponed.

ASHLEY HOLLINGS filed for divorce after she discovered her husband, STANFORD, was canoodling with the Venezuelan party planner who coincidentally organized her fiftieth birthday bash. Rumor has it, Stanford is about to become a father. Ashley intends to drive him to the cleaners and back again. In Stanford's Ferrari, natch.

RAYMOND PRINCE'S used car business is flourishing courtesy of the steady flow of retirees seeking the "Fontainebleau" of forever youth. He and his wife, SANDY, renewed their vows in a lavish ceremony in Las Vegas. Raymond has since been certified as a Red Cross lifeguard and volunteers at a handicapped kids' camp as a swimming instructor. He still refuses to eat seafood.

And, as of this very moment, CLARENCE "WOODY" WOODS and KRISTIN LITTLE, along with SWEETIE, are sailing on the *Sea Sponge* somewhere off the coast of Spain. They are writing a memoir together of their adventures and have already sold the film rights. Part of the proceeds are to be donated, of course, to a worthy environmental charity.